Lynch

Lynch

A Gothik Western

Nancy A. Collins

Cover image © 1998, 2012 by Stephen R. Bissette, used with permission

ISBN: 978-1-5040-1541-7

Distributed in 2015 by Open Road Distribution
345 Hudson Street
New York, NY 10014
www.openroadmedia.com

Dedicated to Clint & Sergio

Lynch

Chapter One

HE WOKE UP DRUNK and reckoned he'd go ahead and stay that way.

It took Johnny Pearl a second to remember where he was. For one brief, sweet moment, he imagined he was dozing on the summer porch, listening to the clatter of buckboards on the cobblestones as they headed for market. But then he opened his eyes and found himself in the shabby backroom of a frontier bar.

Charleston was far away and long ago, replaced by yet another starved-dog town, this one clinging to the edge of the Wyoming territory like a tick. He wasn't sure if it had a name, or even needed one. But at least it had a saloon.

He'd ridden into town two days back, covered in trail dust so thick that from a distance it looked like he was still wearing his old uniform. The first thing he did upon setting foot between the swinging doors of the saloon was call for a bottle of rotgut and a hot bath, which he got toot-sweet.

Pearl wasn't sure if the yokels recognized him. The likeness on the wanted posters wasn't a good one, that much was certain. But they didn't have to know his name to see he was trouble. The way he wore his guns was giveaway enough. And once Pearl knocked off the dust, the color of his clothes left no doubt in even the thickest cowhand's mind that this was a dangerous man.

Johnny Pearl stepped out of the spare room, pausing only long enough to take a deep breath and slick his hair back. The interior of the saloon was close to threadbare, with the bar little more than planks atop sawhorses. A beefy man with a ruddy face sat behind a battered upright piano, diligently hammering away at what might have been "Clementine." Upon catching sight of him, the pianist got to his feet.

"Afternoon, sir. How you feeling today?"

"Like I need a drink."

The piano player nodded his head and hurried behind the bar. Or at least what passed for one in this godforsaken wilderness. At least they had a mirror behind it.

"One whiskey coming right up."

As he turned to pick up the shot glass, Pearl caught sight of himself in the mirror's silvery finish. He was only thirty-one, but you couldn't tell it by looking at him. His dark hair was already graying at the temples, and his eyes resembled coals dropped in a snow bank. The lines about his mouth were hard and sharp, as if they'd been cut into his face with a knife. But then, three years fighting Billy Yank and four years fighting everything else could do that to a man.

Still, thirty-one was a dangerous age for someone like Pearl. The territories were full of half-crazy man-boys with nothing to lose but their lives. When you're seventeen, eighteen years old, you're full of piss and gunpowder, fearless as only those who've never seen death firsthand can be. You're quick to take offense and just as quick to give it.

But once you get into your late twenties—once you've spilled more blood than beer, seen a grown man lie in the mud and wail like a baby while trying to stuff his guts back inside him after he's taken shrapnel, known fear so well you wake up tasting it—that's when things start getting truly dangerous. That's when you're more likely than not to get yourself killed. Not because you're green and shooting before you think, but because you're more apt to think before you shoot.

And, inevitably, with each passing birthday, the reflexes slow a tad more, the joints ache a little sharper. Pearl knew he had a few more years left before rheumatism or the shakes got the better of him, assuming he didn't let his guard down before then.

After all, mercy and a conscience have no place in a gunman's heart. Still, traveling alone as he did, he constantly had to watch his back. Not that he was famous back east like Wild Bill, or Kit Carson or Jesse James, but he had his reputation . . .

"Johnny Pearl!"

He paused, the shot glass halfway to his mouth and glanced in the mirror at the reflection of the farmhand standing behind him. The yokel stood just behind him and to the left, a few feet in from the swinging batwings. The gun strapped to the farmhand's hip was, like the rest of what he wore, too big for him and looked like a hand-me-down. The boy's face was sunburned and spotty, with bright yellow hair that stuck out like straw and made him look even more like a scarecrow.

"I'm a-callin' you out!" the yokel said in a loud voice that cracked halfway through his sentence.

Pearl gave a small sigh and turned from the bar to regard the would-be gunslinger. "Kid, why don't you do us both a favor and go back home and help your daddy get his crops in?" he said, his voice weary but not unkind. Having said his piece, he turned back to his drink. While he sipped at the liquor, he kept his eyes fixed on the mirror.

The kid's face quickly developed hectic blotches of angry red. "Yer yeller, Pearl!" the boy yelled, his voice breaking yet again. "Scart yeller I'll git ya!"

Pearl smiled then. "I'm scared all right, kid. But you only got it half right."

"Yellerbelly!"

The kid pulled his gun and fired at where Pearl was standing at the bar, but the gunman was already moving, throwing himself forward and low. The kid's first shot went wild and shattered the bottle of redeye that had been at Pearl's elbow, sending a shower of glass and brownish liquid across the bar. Pearl had his gun out before he hit the sawdust, automatically returning fire. The kid's feet went out from under him like he'd slipped on dog shit, landing hard on his back, the gun flying from his rawboned hand.

Pearl lay on his belly, his smoking gun clutched tight in his hand. His heart beat fast and the smell of cordite burned his nostrils. It was a full thirty seconds before he was satisfied he hadn't taken a hit.

"Mister? You all right?" The bartender was leaning over him. As he got to his feet, Pearl could see a couple of townies peering in through the door. "Don't you worry none, sir," the bartender said in a low, reassuring voice. "I'll swear to the magistrate when he comes 'round you didn't have no choice in the matter. The boy drew on you, plain and simple."

Pearl stepped forward, looking down at the dead kid sprawled at his feet. Funny, it was only now that the boy was dead that he could see how young he truly was. Still, part of him was surprised, and secretly pleased, that he'd managed to nail the kid right between the eyes.

Pearl motioned to the dead boy. "Do you know who he is—was?"

The bartender nodded. "Looks to be Ezra Sutter's boy, Caleb."

Pearl wiped at his mouth with the back of his hand, which was still gripping the smoking pistol. Try as he might, he couldn't take his eyes off the hole in the kid's forehead. "How old is he?"

"He ain't more than thirteen, I reckon . . ."

Pearl reached inside his waistcoat pocket and pulled out a gold piece, tossing it onto the bar. "I want two bottles of whiskey brought to my room. What's left over is to be put toward burying the boy."

"Y-yes, sir. Anything else?"

"Just see that that I ain't bothered," Pearl said quietly as he stared at Caleb Sutter's blood and brains seeping into the sawdust on the barroom floor. "All I want is to be left to myself."

Chapter Two

THE GUN WAS CALLING TO HIM AGAIN.

Pearl hated when it did that. The gun usually waited until he was drunk or tired or simply sick of it all. It was tricky that way.

Although he had two revolvers, it was always the same one that called out for him: the one with the pearl handle. He'd had the grip custom-made down in New Orleans years ago, back when he had more fire in his belly than whiskey. He could have easily had both pieces fitted that way, but he chose just the one. The one he used the most. His killing iron. A bit of theatrics is what it was. Something for the penny dreadfuls.

But sometimes he wondered if by acknowledging its importance—its unique function—he had not imparted to the weapon a dreadful vitality. After all, it's the sick oyster that has the pearl. It rode heavier on his hip with each passing year, as if fattened by the souls of those it had escorted into the Great Beyond. Or so it seemed in his mind.

Johnny Pearl wasn't sure if he believed in ghosts. But he certainly believed in Evil. Lord knows, he'd done enough of it to recognize it when he heard its voice. And the voice of the gun was Evil indeed.

Like all things made of sin, the gun called to him only when he

7

was weak. As a young man, the possibility of vulnerability had been unimaginable. Perhaps such frailty was the inevitable state of Man. But it all seemed so unfair to him that the Lord should demand perfection, yet leave His children to dwell in perpetual temptation.

Pearl sat on the sole chair in his rented room, drinking by himself, as these thoughts came to him. Not that there was much else for him to do but drink. The one window in the room looked out onto the rear of the stables, permitting a view of churned muck and a couple of bored pigs the blacksmith kept in his backyard.

He had started off drinking out of a glass, but after an hour he'd given up on such niceties and drank the rotgut straight from the bottle. He stared at the unpainted plank walls as if they held the pattern of the world within their knotholes and whorls.

Pearl had come a far piece from his boyhood in the Carolinas—but he was neither proud nor amazed by this. He had been born the scion of a well-respected family. And when the war drums rolled, he had been among the first to enlist. He'd been full of romance and chivalry and other damn fool ideas back then.

He'd fought hard and suffered more physical and emotional wounds than a callow youth eager to teach Billy Yank his place could ever imagine. He'd lost friends beyond number, bearing witness to their death throes in the muck and the mud. He had watched them die every way a man could: bravely, cruelly, fearfully, foolishly . . . uselessly.

And when it was all over, he'd made his way back to the place of his birth to find his home burned, his family dead of the fever that had tagged along after the invading troops like a hungry dog. He'd gone a little crazy then, like a lot of young men who'd fought for Dixie and seen it come to naught. Some folks would say he was still a little crazy. Even him.

Seeing how there was nothing for him, and that the world he had once known was never to return again, he set out to make a new life for himself. However, he didn't have the temperament to become a settler. Nor did he have the wherewithal to set himself up in business. Without family or friends to temper his anger, anchor his feet or salve his soul—the way of the gun seemed as good as any for a man of his background. Perhaps better than most. And since there wasn't much that Johnny Pearl knew how to do except kill his fellow man, that's what he did.

For the first few years, it wasn't a half-bad life. There was excitement and thrills, like those he'd known during the war.

And although there was a great deal danger in the life he led, there was also freedom. But as the killings started to add up, the excitement began to be replaced by weariness, the wildness became more and more like madness, and the freedom a trap.

And, to make matters worse, the gun started talking to him.

When he first started hearing the call of the gun, its voice was far weaker than it was now. But as his resolve lessened, the gun's voice grew stronger, more distinct. At first he could not quite identify its voice. But now he recognized it not to be just one voice, but many, woven together like the braid of a rope. The voice of the gun was comprised of the voices of all those he had killed, all those he had wronged, all who were lost to him.

Its voice cajoled and chided and ridiculed and argued, the myriad voices losing their individuality, merging and melding until it became a wordless, plaintive wail, like that of the siren of legend who lured ancient sailors to their deaths.

The gun only wanted one thing. The same thing Pearl wanted, really. Peace. But there was only one way it could ever know *true* peace. And that was if he used the gun one last time . . .

"Don't!"

There was a girl standing in the door of his room, her eyes showing more white than a billiard ball. She was young, dressed in a gingham skirt, with long dark hair pulled back in a single braid that fell almost to her waist. She carried a fresh slop jar in one hand, a skeleton key in the other.

Johnny Pearl wondered why she looked so frightened, and then he realized he had the muzzle of the gun pressed against his temple.

"Pardon me, ma'am," he said thickly, lowering the weapon. "Didn't mean to scare you none."

The girl hesitated for a moment, as if trying to decide whether to flee the room.

"You're not going to kill yourself, are you?" she asked.

Pearl shrugged, but did not reholster the gun. "Who would it matter to if I did?"

"It would matter to me," she replied quietly.

Pearl squinted at the girl, struggling to bring her into focus through the haze of rotgut. "You Injun?"

Her cheeks colored slightly. "Half. My mama was Cheyenne."

"No shame in that," Pearl smiled gently. "My grandma was Cherokee."

He was suddenly aware of just how wretched he must look, with his unshaven jaw and filthy hair. He returned the gun to its holster, its voice strangely silent for the first time in years.

"What's your name, gal?" he rasped.

"Katie. Katie Small Dove."

"That's a right pretty name." He cocked his head to one side. "You ain't scared of me, are you?"

"No, sir. I ain't."

"Why is that? You know who I am—what I done?"

"Yes, sir, I know all them things. But I still ain't scared of you. I seen bad men before—more than my share. I know what they're like, and you ain't like them. I seen how you tried to keep from havin' to kill that boy. A bad man—a real bad man—wouldn't have bothered with that. He'd have shot that boy soon as look at him. So's that's why I ain't scared. Leastwise not for myself. I'm more scared for you than of you."

Pearl smiled and got up from the chair, motioning for her to take his place. "Come sit and visit with me a while, Katie. It's been a long time since I talked to anyone with horse sense."

She glanced over her shoulder. "I got work I need to do . . . ."

"Pretty please? With sugar on top?"

Katie giggled. It was a sweet, natural sound, like birdsong in the trees. "I guess I can talk for a lit'l while, mister," she said, stepping into the room.

"Call me Johnny," he said.

"All right—Johnny," she replied, beaming him a smile that could raise the dead.

Chapter Three

IT WAS AUTUMN, and even though the days were still warm, it didn't take a trained eye to spot winter approaching. The last couple of mornings Pearl had awoken to find a thin skin of ice covering the rain barrel outside the cabin door, and frost in the shadow of the rocks.

It had been over a year since Johnny Pearl did something he had never thought possible—traded in the black garb of the gunslinger for the buckskins and homespun of a settler. And he had yet to regret one minute of a single day since then, despite the long hours and hard work.

He could take no credit for his rebirth; it was all Katie's doing. She was the one who had given him the strength and incentive to turn his feet from the destructive path he had walked so long. Her love had raised him up from the shadows, just as Jesus brought Lazarus back from the Land of the Dead. Pearl had given himself up for lost, but she still managed to guide him back to the land of the living, the land of hope. She was a miracle worker, that woman.

Although there was no proper preacher to be had, Johnny Pearl considered Katie joined to him as surely as Eve had been to Adam. Since there was no preacher to be had, they had ridden into the foothills one day, and, when their horses had climbed as high as they could go, Pearl took her hand in his and shouted up at the sky: "Lord! This here's Johnny Pearl! I'm taking Katie Small Dove for my wife!" He figured that was probably as official as they could get, given the circumstances.

Now that Katie was carrying their first child, Pearl felt as if he had been blessed by God Himself. For the first time since the war had come into his life, he could look to the future and see something besides smoke and ashes. As a symbol of his rebirth, he took his old clothes and the pearl-handled pistol and buried them underneath the cabin's flagstones.

When Katie asked him why he didn't just burn the clothes and throw the gun in the river, he shook his head. "I'm not proud of what I used to be, but there's no denying it, either. I need to be reminded of what I was once was so I won't turn back into it again."

He and Katie made their home in a cabin abandoned by a faint-hearted settler, and their closest neighbor was ten miles away, the nearest town nearly a hundred. All of which was fine and dandy, as far as Pearl was concerned. Their existence was humble but adequate; Katie tended a small garden near the cabin—mostly corn and squash—while he ranged for antelope, shorthorn and rabbit. For those few items they couldn't make themselves, Pearl took bear, coyote and panther skins with him on his rare trips into town.

However, just because their nearest white neighbor was a two-hour ride away, that didn't mean they were total recluses. They received occasional visits from some of Katie's Indian relatives, one of her favorites being her elder cousin, Ohkom Kakit, known to the whites as Little Wolf.

Little Wolf was a respected war chief among the Cheyenne, which guaranteed the Pearls a certain amount of protection—at least from the natives. It wasn't an easy life, but it was a free one, and for that Johnny Pearl was thankful. He had never thought he would settle down the way he had, but damned if every evening he couldn't be found sitting on the modest porch of his cabin, enjoying a quiet smoke as he contemplated the land as the sun went down.

He had the river running at his door, the rolling expanse of the plains on one hand, the mountains stretched out like sleeping giants on the other, and a sky like a great blue bowl turned upside down overhead. How could he not look out on all that and not think that this was indeed the best of all worlds, these the finest of all days, and that it would never end?

He was wrong, of course.

They appeared without warning—a neat trick, given the terrain—while Pearl was busy chopping wood. One minute he was by himself, the next he was surrounded by snorting, stamping ponies. Normally a settler on the high plains would be alarmed by the sight of several armed Cheyenne warriors, but Johnny Pearl merely smiled in recognition.

"Greetings, cousin," he said, setting aside his axe so none of the braves accompanying his wife's kinsman might get the wrong idea.

"Greetings, Johnny Pearl," Little Wolf responded.

There was something in the old chief's voice that gave him pause. Pearl glanced at the assembled Cheyenne. Even though their skin was darker and their uniforms different, he still knew soldiers when he saw them.

Katie emerged from the cabin, wiping cornmeal from her hands. "To what do we owe the honor of this visit, *Ohkom Kakit*?" she asked.

Little Wolf shook his head. "This is no visit, Small Dove. I come to warn you."

Johnny frowned and put his arm about his wife's shoulder. "Warn us? About what?"

Little Wolf glanced at his men, and then took a deep breath. "Three moons past there was a great battle between the white man and the red man along the Greasy Grass."

"You mean Custer," Johnny Pearl said grimly. "I heard tell of it last time I was in town."

"Yes. The yellow-hair," Little Wolf nodded. "It was a great victory for the Cheyenne and the Sioux. We counted great coup against the pony soldiers."

"You were there?" Pearl asked in surprise.

Little Wolf nodded and smiled crookedly, trying to keep his pride from showing. "It was a great fight. But now the whites are angry and seek to hunt us down and punish us for this thing."

"The U.S. Army don't take kindly to gettin' whupped," Pearl sighed. "I can tell you that first-hand."

"The pony soldiers are rounding up all Cheyenne, all Sioux—warriors, women, children, grandfathers—all of us! They seek to lock us away from our hunting grounds and our sacred places as punishment for daring to fight. They will try and take Katie away from you, Johnny Pearl."

"Why would they do that? She ain't full-blooded. Besides, she's my wife."

"Perhaps you are right, Johnny Pearl," Little Wolf conceded. "You know the mind of your people better than I do. But you would be wise to leave this place and come with us. We are headed for Dull Knife's village. There we stand a better chance against the pony soldiers when they come."

"We appreciate the concern, Little Wolf," Pearl said. "But we're staying put. Besides, Katie is in no condition to travel." He smiled and patted his wife's swollen belly.

"All the more reason to leave," Little Wolf frowned.

Katie glanced anxiously at her husband but said nothing. Seeing the fear in his kinswoman's eyes, the Cheyenne chief's grim demeanor softened.

"Do not be frightened, little cousin. Your husband is a good man and a fine warrior. Farewell, blood-of-my-blood. And many blessings on your child."

"I thank you, *Ohkom Kakit*, "Katie replied, blinking back a tear. "You're welcome to stay here as long as you like."

Little Wolf shook his head and pointed to the clear, cloudless sky on the horizon. "We must go. There is a storm coming."

Two days after Little Wolf and his followers left, the storm arrived.

It wasn't a storm that brought with it thunder and high winds and hailstones. No, the storm that bore down of Johnny and Katie Pearl was a mortal one—the kind that rains fire and hot lead.

Pearl had just finished milking the nanny goat and was bringing the pail into the house when the thunder rose through this boots. It had been a long time since he last felt anything like that—but it wasn't something a man could forget. Many men on horseback were coming their way—riding hard.

Katie was in the front yard, throwing feed to the chickens. When she saw the look in her husband's eyes, she let her apron drop and ran into the cabin, re-emerging seconds later with the carbine.

"Git in th' house and stay there!" Pearl ordered as he loaded the Winchester.

Katie hesitated, placing a hand on her husband's arm. "Perhaps it is only my cousin . . . ."

Pearl shook his head, his mouth set in a grim line. "Whoever they are, they ain't Cheyenne!" Katie gave his arm one last squeeze and disappeared inside the cabin just as a horse cleared the rise.

Most whites in the Wyoming and Dakota territories heaved a sigh of relief when they saw the U.S. Cavalry. Johnny Pearl wasn't one of them. He'd spent too many years shooting at blue uniforms—and being shot at by them—to find their presence comforting. He watched uneasily as the squadron of troopers, roughly thirty in all, made its way toward his cabin. As the soldiers drew closer, Pearl stepped off the porch into the dooryard but did not lower his weapon.

The squadron's scout trotted his mount forward to where Pearl was standing, lifting his empty hand in greeting. There was something about him Pearl didn't trust. He fidgeted in his saddle too much, like he had a ferret down his pants.

"Howdy," the scout said, looking about. "Where's John Myerling?"

"He pulled up stakes and went back to St. Paul. I took over his cabin," Johnny replied.

"That a fact?" The scout glanced in the direction of the soldiers, but Pearl couldn't make out who he was looking at. "Have you seen any Injuns?"

"Sure, I seen Injuns. See 'em all the time. Now get off my land."

The scout twitched in his saddle again, his eyes narrowing. "You sure got a smart mouth for a sodbuster."

"I *said* get off my land," Pearl replied, his voice hard as an iron bar.

15

The scout's eyes narrowed a split second before he reached for his holster, which was all the warning Pearl needed to step forward and jam his rifle directly into the other man's crotch. The scout yanked his hand back like his gun had turned into a red-hot poker.

"Y-you're bluffing, honyocker," the scout sneered.

"I *never* bluff."

There was something in Pearl's voice that that made the scout decide not to push his luck. He licked his lips nervously and fidgeted even more in his saddle.

"What the hell is going on here?" boomed an angry voice. An officer dressed in the uniform of a Cavalry captain rode forward. He was a big man, the way trees are big and rocks are big. His shoulders were as wide as an ax handle and his hands could easily hide Bibles. However, the captain's most intimidating feature was not his sheer physical size, but the wavy mass of red hair that fell below his shoulders, and the matching beard and mustaches he wore combed out over his chest, which made him look like a lion. His stern face was burned by the sun, and his pale eyes were a startling contrast to the darker blue of his uniform and the vibrancy of his hair. "Put that weapon down, farmer!" the captain barked. It was clear he was used to being obeyed, be it by soldiers or civilians.

"Like hell I will!" Johnny snapped in reply. "And who might you be?"

"Captain Antioch Drake, United States Cavalry. Now do as I say, sodbuster, or I'll forget I'm talking to a white man and have my men open fire!"

Pearl glanced at Drake, then stepped back, lowering his gun. What he'd seen looking at him through Drake's eyes was all too familiar. He'd known men like him during the war: bloody-minded and scarlet-handed, incapable of separating friend from foe, soldier from civilian. Quantrill had been one such monster. If the war had taught Pearl one thing, it was that a bastard's a bastard, whether suited up in blue or gray. And what he saw before him was a bastard in a blue suit.

"That's better," Drake said. "Now—are you going to answer the question my scout put to you or not? Did you see Injuns pass this way a day or two ago?"

"What makes you think there's been Injuns through here recently?" Johnny asked, trying his best to sidestep the question.

"We've been following their trail—and it lead us to you," Drake responded. "Now—did you or did you not see Injuns passing through?"

"What do you want them for?"

"They were amongst those murderin' redskins responsible for the massacre of the Seventh Cavalry under Lieutenant Colonel George Custer at Little Big Horn," Drake replied, his tone reverent.

"Do tell," Pearl said, spitting in the dirt.

Drake seemed surprised by Pearl's blatant indifference. "You *do* know about what happened at Little Big Horn, don't you?"

Pearl shrugged. "Yeah. I know. But that still don't explain why *y'all* are on my property, askin' *me* questions about Injuns."

Drake's scowl deepened. "That's some accent you've got there. You're not from around here, are you?"

"Funny. I was gonna say th' same about y'all," Pearl grunted.

Drake leaned back in his saddle, his pale irises seeming to disappear against the whites of his eye. "You wouldn't be lyin' to me about them Injuns just to make up for Stonewall Jackson, would you, Reb?"

Johnny Pearl's cheeks burned, but he would be damned if he let this Union-suited son of a bitch get his goat. Still, he could not keep a waver of anger from entering his voice when he spoke. "How can I lie if I ain't tole y'all nothin'! Now, get off my land! I got better things to do than to spend my day jawin' with Yankees!"

One minute the cavalry officer's hand was empty, the next the muzzle of his Colt was pressed against Pearl's temple. There was no way Pearl could bring the carbine up in time to squeeze off a shot without Drake putting his brains on the ground, and both men knew it.

"Who's in the cabin?" Drake growled.

Johnny struggled to speak around what felt like a rock wedged in his throat. "J-just my wife."

Drake's eyes narrowed into ice-blue slits. "I thought you said you was alone, Reb."

"I didn't say *nothin'* about bein' alone!" Johnny protested. "Y'all are just twistin' everything I say!"

"We'll just see about that," Drake replied. He motioned with his free hand for a couple of his men to come forward. "Take his weapon, and see that he stays out from underfoot."

With Drake's service revolver cocked and aimed just above his right ear, Pearl was helpless to prevent the troopers from confiscating his rifle then roughly binding his hands behind his back. Satisfied Pearl was no longer a hindrance; Drake holstered his weapon and turned to speak to his junior officer.

"Lieutenant Barnes! I want that cabin searched!"

"Yes, sir!" Barnes barked, saluting Drake. He promptly dismounted and motioned several troopers to do the same. Guns drawn, they advanced on the cabin.

Johnny Pearl was no stranger to terror. Sometimes it seemed he was born knowing it. But before now, the fear he had experienced on the battlefield and in shootouts had always been for his own life. None of what he had undergone before had come close to preparing him for the sick dread that overcame him when he heard his wife scream.

"*Katie!*" Pearl shouted, struggling to break free of the troopers holding him. He wanted to scream, explode, turn himself inside out if need be—anything but let the bastards see his fear. "Don't you *dare* touch her, you stinkin' Yankee bastards!"

"Mind your mouth, Reb!" snarled one of the troopers as he smashed Pearl in the face with his gun butt. Through the stars exploding behind his eyes, Pearl saw his wife being dragged out of the cabin.

"Here y'go, Captain," the scout said. "Weren't no one but her in the house."

Drake took in Katie's long dark braid, high cheekbones, dusky skin and almond-shaped eyes, then turned to glower at his captive disapprovingly. "I thought you said there were no Injuns around here."

"I ain't said no such thing!" Pearl snarled, spitting out a mouthful of blood. "Besides, Katie ain't full Cheyenne."

"Even a *drop* of heathen blood is enough to mark her as theirs!" Drake sniffed. "She'll have go on the reservation—the brat, too."

"No! She's my *wife*, damn it! That's my baby she's carryin'!"

Drake fixed him with a look of utter contempt. "Which makes you a squaw man—and as such, no better than a dog!"

Pearl lunged forward, his teeth bared in pure, murder-hot rage. If the troopers had not been holding him back, he would have leapt onto Drake and taken him off his saddle like a mountain cat bringing down an antelope. Instead, all he got for his trouble was his own rifle butt slammed across the back of his head, dropping him to the ground.

As he lay writhing in the dirt, clutching his skull, he heard a shriek of pain and surprise from the scout; "*Jesus H. Christ!* That Injun bitch damn near bit off my finger!"

Pearl raised his head in time to see Katie running as fast as she could away from the soldiers, but her belly was getting in her way. Within seconds the mounted troopers had surrounded her. They were laughing and making whooping noises, waving their hats at her as if she were no more than an errant cow they were trying to return to the herd. Katie dashed frantically to and fro, clutching her belly. She tried to find an opening in the tightening ring of champing horses.

It all happened so fast, so horribly, horribly fast. One moment Katie was calling out her husband's name amid the chaos and the churning dust—the next she was under the horses' hooves. Pearl wasn't aware he was screaming until Lieutenant Barnes put a fist in his gut to shut him up.

Barnes massaged his knuckles as he watched Pearl gasp and choke for air. "What do we do with him, Captain?"

Drake's eyes were as cold and unyielding as sapphires. "Make him an example for all those who would pollute the white race. Lynch him. Burn the cabin, while you're at it."

"Yes, sir!" Barnes responded, saluting sharply.

As his captors dragged him toward the nearest tree, Pearl felt as hollow as a dry gourd. It was as if they had reached down his gullet and yanked his soul out by the roots. Death, no matter how violent or unjust, was preferable to life in a world without his Katie.

The last thing Johnny Pearl saw before they chased the horse out from under him was the sight of his world in ruins: his house ablaze, his wife's body sprawled in the bloody dust, and the scout bending over her, knife in hand.

19

Chapter Four

AS THE COVERED WAGON made its way across the high plains, each jounce of its wheels made the utensils hanging in the back rattle like cowbells. If the old man perched on the driver's box noticed the incessant clatter, he did not show it. Instead, his eye was fixed on the plume of smoke on the horizon. On the side of the canvas canopy was painted in bold, somewhat faded script:

Dr. Mirablis Wondrous Elixir Re-Vitae $1
(50 cents to Veterans & Widows).

"Pompey!" Dr. Mirablis croaked. "Come front!"

The head of a middle-aged Negro, the hair liberally laced with gray, popped out from behind the canvas flap separating the driver's seat from the interior of the wagon.

"Take the reins on Alastor," Mirablis wheezed. "We're getting close. I must check on the elixir."

Pompey nodded his understanding and moved aside, holding back the canvas so the old man could climb back into the wagon's bed. He then seated himself on the driver's box and took up the coal black horse's reins. The beast flared its nostrils and rolled its eyes. It could smell death mixed with the smoke wafted their way by the wind. As could they all.

Pompey flicked the reins across the horse's flanks, forcing it to move faster.

"Would you look at that," Dr. Mirablis sighed, shaking his head in amazement as he viewed what was left of the homestead. "They even shot the nanny goat."

Twenty-four hours ago, this had been a place where people lived, worked and planned for the future. Now it was a scene of carnage. The cabin still smoldered. Although the roof had fallen in, the stone chimney still stood, but little else remained. The modest garden had been trampled into the dirt, and the livestock slaughtered and left to rot. Such barbarity was nothing new to a man who had survived the chaos of the Napoleonic Wars, but it still grieved him all the same.

Pompey grunted as he helped the old man down off the driver's box. Mirablis was bent with age and walked with a cane.

His hair was white and thin as cobwebs. His scalp was dappled with the same spots that covered his wrinkled hands. Despite his advanced years, there was an intensity in his eyes—the kind found only in those of fierce intellect and even fiercer determination.

"Bloodthirsty savages," Mirablis muttered under his breath as he shuffled through a litter of trampled chickens. The old man paused and pointed with his cane at something lying in the dirt nearby. "What's that?" As they drew closer, Mirablis's eyes widened and he began hobbling faster, despite Pompey's attempts to keep him balanced. With a snarl of impatience, the old man yanked his arm free of his servant's grasp and knelt beside the body of Katie Pearl. He grimaced in disgust and clucked his tongue. "This one is of no use to me—her skull has been smashed, as you can plainly tell, since some barbarian saw fit to take the poor thing's scalp! Such a waste! And in the later stages of pregnancy as well." Mirablis's eyes dimmed, as the fire held within them was turned inward. A moment later he gestured for Pompey to help him back on his feet. "Still, if there was a mother," he said. "There has to be a father . . . ."

His companion gently touched Mirablis's shoulder and pointed to a flock of carrion crows circling a copse of trees that lined the nearby river.

"Ah, trusty Pompey!" Mirablis smiled, flashing his wooden and ivory dentures. "Ever my eyes and ears, old friend! Come, let us hurry! I can only pray those damnable birds haven't had their way with our new friend!"

They found the body of Johnny Pearl hanging from the stout limb of a cottonwood tree. The tree was within sight of the homestead's front yard. Though the dead man was not visible from the cabin, the lynched man's final view from his unenviable vantage had been of his home ablaze and his wife's mutilated carcass. However, what made Mirablis cry out in outrage was the sight of a large crow perched atop the hanged man's head, its inky claws buried deep in his scalp.

"Pompey! Get that wretched thing *off* him!"

Producing a slingshot from his back pocket, the mute quickly snatched up a small rock from the ground and sent the missile flying at the bird. The crow abandoned its grisly perch with an angry caw. Mirablis positioned himself directly under the hanged man's feet, peering up into his distorted face.

"We're in luck, Pompey! The scavengers didn't get too much of a head start. It's a good thing winter's on its way—the flies should be mostly inactive by now, so there won't be much in the way of infestation to worry about." The old man laughed and held up a shaking hand. "Look at me, Pompey! I'm trembling like a school girl!" Mirablis's giddy smile was quickly replaced by a grimmer manner. "Go fetch Sasquatch! We'll need him to transport our new friend here into the pouch. I'll stay here and play scarecrow until your return."

Pompey nodded and hurried back to the wagon. He rapped his knuckles loudly on its wooden side. After a moment, the tailgate dropped open and the canvas flaps that covered the rear were thrown back, and something that once was a man emerged into the cold light of a September afternoon on the high plains.

The thing was tall and not exactly put together the way a human is supposed to look. Its left arm was shorter than the right—or was it that the right arm was longer than the left? The legs seemed to be equally mismatched, with one foot severely pigeon-toed while the other pointed straight. Scars of various lengths and widths crisscrossed the creature's exposed flesh, giving it the appearance of a walking crazy quilt.

Though it was naked save for a leather loincloth, and was lean as a winter wolf, the creature did not seem to notice the chill wind blowing from the mountains. Besides its one garment and the color of its skin, the only other telltale sign that the creature called Sasquatch had once been an American Indian was its long black hair, which hung loose down its back.

Sasquatch watched Pompey's hands as the Negro spoke in the sign language of the plains people, then nodded. He then turned and reached into the wagon, pulling out a seven-foot-long homemade ladder as if it weighed no more than a child's toy.

Mirablis rubbed his hands together anxiously as he paced back and forth beneath the swaying body of the hanged man. He brightened immediately upon spotting Pompey approaching with the ladder. A few steps behind the mute shambled the figure of Sasquatch, the leather pouch folded under his shorter left arm, the cask of elixir under the longer right arm.

"We must hurry!" Mirablis said breathily. Though the weather was somewhat brisk, he mopped his brow with a silk handkerchief. "We were exceptionally fortunate this time, as I believe our friend here has been inconvenienced less than twelve hours. But time is still of the essence!"

Pompey placed the ladder against the cottonwood and began to climb, while Mirablis supervised Sasquatch as he unrolled the pouch. It was made of oiled cloth and resembled nothing so much as a wine-skin, except that it was six feet long and three feet wide. At one end was a huge stopper fashioned from wood wrapped in treated leather.

Pompey made a grunting noise, signaling the others that he was ready. Sasquatch moved to position himself directly under the swaying feet of the hanged man. After a few slices from Pompey's buck knife, the body dropped from the tree like strange fruit, directly into Sasquatch's waiting arms. With surprising grace and gentleness for a creature of such ungainly appearance, Sasquatch laid the corpse on the ground at Mirablis's feet and proceeded to undress it.

The old man studied the body with a critical eye, then nodded his head and smiled. "This is even better than I hoped!" he said, pointing to the corpse's livid but otherwise unmarked flesh. "From all outward appearances, our friend here was in exemplary physical condition before he was so rudely inconvenienced." Mirablis waved his cane in warning as Pompey began to pry off the noose cinched into the dead man's neck. "Leave that for later! It is too deeply embedded in the flesh to be removed on the scene."

Having finished his inspection, Mirablis stepped back and motioned for his servants to proceed with their duties. While Pompey held the neck of the giant flask upright, Sasquatch slid the body through the man-sized opening as easily as a mother might put a sleepy child to bed.

Once the body was fully inside the pouch, the plug was put in place, and then driven home by Sasquatch with one swift rap from a cooper's mallet. At the top of the plug was a hole the width of a man's finger, down which Pompey ran one end of a length of canvas tubing. The other end was attached to a spigot at the bottom of the cask of elixir. With a turn of the spigot, the elixir flowed through the tubing and into the watertight container.

While they waited for the pouch to fill, Sasquatch moved the wagon closer to the scene and made a fire, over which he warmed a small bucket of tar. When the pouch was filled enough that it sloshed upon Mirablis nudging it with his cane, the tubing was removed and the hole sealed with the hot tar. As Pompey disconnected the spigot, a small amount of viscous greenish yellow fluid spurted forth onto the ground.

"Careful, fool!" Mirablis snapped, bringing his cane down on the mute's shoulder with surprising force. Pompey did not even flinch. "My elixir is far too valuable to waste on worms!" The old man looked around, frowning. "Where in the name of Perdition did Sasquatch get off to?"

Pompey pointed in the direction of the ruined cabin. The patch-work creature was kneeling beside the dead woman, making passes with his mismatched hands over the body. Part of Sasquatch had been a shaman, but just how much of him Mirablis wasn't sure. As a man of science, Mirablis tended to dismiss such silliness. But he had to admit he found some aspects of the medicine man within his servant useful, so he allowed him his superstitions. After all, revived from the dead or not, he was still a red savage.

"Sasquatch! It's time to go!" Mirablis shouted, "Our new friend needs to get situated!"

Muttering under his breath about heathen tomfoolery, the old man returned to where Pompey was standing guard over the pouch. A few seconds later, Sasquatch reappeared and lifted it and placed it in the back of the wagon as easily as a farmer hefting a ten-pound sack of seed. After making sure the container and its occupant were firmly secured, Sasquatch crawled back into rear of the wagon, closing the tailgate behind him.

Mirablis paused to glance up at the sky as Pompey helped him back onto the driver's box. "It'll be dark soon. We better get out while the getting's good, my friends," he observed. "The less time spent at the scene of a crime, the better—whether it's of our making or not. Still, not a bad day's work, if I don't say so myself."

Chapter Five

THE COVERED WAGON TRAVELED for three days and nights without pause. On the morning of the fourth day, Mirablis and hi peculiar entourage arrived at their destination, hidden within the forbidding wilderness of the Grand Tetons; from a distance, I looked like nothing more than a cabin pressed close against the side of a foothill. But what appeared to be an isolated shack was actually camouflage for the entrance to a large cavern.

The cabin's furnishings were exceptionally modest. Indeed, the only evidence that someone other than a mountain man lived there was the walnut and glass bookcase in the corner crammed full of medical texts and other, more arcane volumes, written in German, Latin and Greek.

The door set in the back wall of the cabin opened onto the cave. The cave extended far into the hillside and had natural ventilation, a floor that was relatively level and access to an underground spring. Mirablis was not the first to have found it advantageous, judging from the flint arrow heads and broken bowls they'd found scattered among the stalagmites.

When Mirablis accidentally stumbled across the cave years ago, he realized it would be the perfect location for his experiments. He had grown weary of spending so much of his time and energy looking over his shoulder. He could no longer count how many times he had been on the verge of a major breakthrough, only to abandon his laboratory because of some snooping neighbor or meddling constable.

He had learned from poor Viktor's hapless example never to arouse the scrutiny of outsiders—and to always erase his mistakes before they could call attention to themselves. Now, for the first time in fifty years, Mirablis was free to continue his work without fear of discovery and censure—and what progress he had made!

It was here, hidden from the prying eyes of a distrustful and ignorant public, that Mirablis worked to free mankind from the inconvenience of mortality. There was no doubt in his mind that in the centuries to come, this wretched hovel would be made into a shrine greater than those in Rome, Bethlehem or Mecca. A shrine dedicated to the genius that struggled so mightily in order that mankind might know Life Without End.

But those days were yet to come, and he still had much to do before they would arrive.

While he had far surpassed his notorious colleague, Mirablis had yet to produce a suitable enough subject that would allow him to unveil his discovery to the world at large. With something as profoundly earthshaking as the death of Death, one had to be absolutely perfect, or it was all for naught. Viktor had proven that, if nothing else.

While Pompey unharnessed the wagon and Sasquatch unloaded their new friend, Mirablis busied himself by starting a fire in the cabin's potbellied stove. While neither Pompey nor Sasquatch seemed to notice the cold, the same could not be said for their master.

"Wait, you heathen fool!" Mirablis shouted irritably as Sasquatch lurched toward the cave entrance with his precious burden. "You might be able to see in the dark, but I require light!"

Sasquatch came to a halt and glanced over his crooked shoulder at Mirablis. In the dim light, the whites of the Indian's eyes glowed with a pale greenish yellow luminescence. The patched-together Indian waited patiently as his creator fumbled with an oil lantern and a box of brimstones.

Pompey stepped unhesitatingly into the stygian darkness of the cavern, the lantern held in one hand while he led his elderly master with the other. The floor of the cavern sloped gently beneath their feet for a few steps, and then leveled out again. As Pompey lifted his arm higher, the light from the lantern struck the glass walls of the tank.

At first glance, it resembled nothing so much as an oversized aquarium. It stood on long, ornate copper legs, the feet of which resembled the claws of lions, and had a burnished lid held in place by tension screws. It was four feet wide, ten feet deep and seven feet long, with side panels made from a greenish-colored glass several inches thick. Through this glass could be glimpsed gallons of the good doctor's special elixir. Along one side of the tank was a raised wooden platform, atop which was situated what passed for Mirablis' operating theater.

While Pompey hurried about lighting crude pitch torches in order to provide more light, Sasquatch stumped its graceless way up the thirteen stairs that lead to the gallows-like platform, then carefully placed his burden onto the operating table. He then loosened the tension screws holding the lid in place and lifted it using a block and tackle.

Once the lid was removed, an elaborate cat's cradle of leather straps was visible just below the surface of the viscous fluid. Pompey then removed the plug with a chisel and, with a practiced movement, Sasquatch expertly decanted the contents of the pouch into the tank.

The body of the hanged man landed in the cradle of leather strips with all the grace of a dead mackerel striking the dock.

For a man several days dead, his color was surprisingly good, and his flesh was pliant. Using a winch attached to the side of tank, Pompey cranked the cradle closer to the surface. Upon putting on a pair of canvas gloves, the mute arranged the corpse's tangled limbs so they were in a rough semblance of natural rest.

"Don't touch that!" Mirablis snapped as his servant tested the cinch on the noose. "I don't need you accidentally damaging the poor bastard's voice box anymore than it has been already!"

Mirablis looked over the edge of the tank from his perch atop his stepladder. He had abandoned the lantern in favor of a miner's headlamp, its wavering candlelight reflected and intensified by the mirror directly behind it. After slipping on a pair of gloves, the doctor gently palpitated the dead man's throat, and then smiled. "Good! Our friend is merely inconvenienced by a broken neck, not a shattered larynx or crushed windpipe. Whoever handled the lynching knew what they were doing, that much is for certain."

Mirablis produced a scalpel from his pocket and quickly sliced through the rope. With a disgusted snort, he tossed the severed noose onto the floor of the platform, where it lay like a perverse umbilical cord. "Now . . . let's see about that eye," he muttered, turning the damaged portion of the corpse's face toward the light.

The head lolled like a rag doll's on its snapped neck. Mirablis frowned at the punctured eyeball and exposed optic muscles and clucked his tongue in mock reproof. "I'm afraid it will *have* to go, my friend! But I believe I have a suitable replacement in stock—although I'm not certain as to its color. Still—beggars can not be choosers, eh?"

Chuckling to himself over that particular witticism, Mirablis stepped down from his ladder and motioned for his servants to reseal the tank.

"There is much to be done before we can revive our new friend. But first, I must avail myself of a nap and a hot meal! Would it not have been better for God to have slept before Creation, rather than after, Pompey?" Mirablis yawned, massaging his lower back. "Think of all the trouble that would have been avoided!"

Pompey merely grunted as he helped his aged master down the stairs of the platform. If there was anything to be read in the silent Negro's eyes, their phosphorescent glow obscured it.

Chapter Six

MIRABLIS PREPARED FOR THE REVIVIFICATION of his newest subject as he always did: b going over his notes and journals—an those of his dear colleague, destroyed so long ago by the forces he sought to control. There was a great deal of inspiration to be found in Viktor's writings. But Mirablis had learned as much—if not more—from his friend's failures than he did his successes.

Poor Viktor. He had indeed been brilliant—his mind shining like a star in the wilderness. In the decades since his death, Mirablis had yet to find another man with which he could discourse as an equal. However, Viktor's one failing was his tendency to fixate simply on achieving a goal. He was never good at making contingency plans in case things did not quite work out as he had hoped. And in the end, his myopic optimism cost him dearly.

Of course, Mirablis was far more forgiving of Viktor's faults now that he was dead. During his life, these differences eventually lead to their falling out. But that was all so long ago, so far away. What were such petty jealousies and disagreements now? Viktor may have realized his goal first, but it was Mirablis who had refined it—and repeated it—and one day soon he would be able to restore his old friend's reputation to the honor it once knew.

He had no doubt that the accounts of his late friend's experiments and his subsequent bad end were grossly inaccurate, if not actually fashioned out of whole cloth, in an attempt to feed the overheated imaginations of shopkeepers' daughters. It galled him to think that all of his friend and mentor's hard work had come to was a slander on the family name and fodder for a thrill-mongering, ill-born wife of a decadent poet.

But enough of that foolishness. He had more weighty duties to attend to. Mirablis pushed himself away from the table and shuffled over to the sea chest he kept under his bed. He groaned aloud as he bent on arthritic knees and opened the lid, revealing an array of sealed jars of varying sizes and shapes. After a quick inventory, he chose a smallish jar containing a pair of eyes, then closed the lid.

Mirablis moved far more spryly now that he was home. Traveling took a serious toll on his aged system, affecting everything from his sleep to his digestion. Unfortunately, there was no way he could continue his work without leaving the security and familiarity of his sanctum. He certainly couldn't send Pompey and Sasquatch out into the world unsupervised. The very thought was enough to give him the shivers.

He opened the second door of the cabin and crossed the threshold into his subterranean kingdom. The interior of the cavern was now illuminated by strategically placed torches and lanterns, revealing a series of ropes stretched between the outcroppings of rock that served as guideposts in case of blackouts. From where he stood, Mirablis could see Pompey and Sasquatch preparing the operating platform for surgery. The tank had been unsealed, its lid dangling from the block and tackle rigged above it from a gibbet-like support.

Upon noticing Mirablis's approach, Pompey put aside the straight razor he had been using to shave the corpse's head and hurried down the steps to escort his aged master onto the platform. As he was helped into his surgical gown, Mirablis scanned the body laid out before him on the operating table with a discerning eye.

Despite being dead for nearly a week, the cadaver was in wondrous shape, thanks largely to the elixir re-vitae. The limbs were still supple, the muscles pliant, yet not softened by decay. If not for the grotesquely unnatural angle of his head, the hanged man could easily be mistaken for asleep. Mirablis clucked his tongue upon seeing a darkish fluid seeping from the body's mouth and nose. He made a mental note to drain the bowels in order to prevent the subject from inhaling his own filth upon revival.

He squeezed and flexed the corpse's arms and legs to make sure there was no muscular decay or contraction in the limbs, then moved the arms so that they hung over the ends of the table, allowing the blood to drain into the vessels and expand them as much as possible. He then took a small wooden headrest and placed it under the back of the subject's skull so that the head was elevated above the chest, to avoid discoloration in the head and neck tissues.

Pompey stepped forward and presented a silver tray on which operating tools were arranged. Mirablis picked up one of the surgical knives and, without hesitation, began to cut away the skin over the left common carotid. Once it was exposed, he skillfully severed it and lifted a portion of the artery out of the body and quickly inserted a metal cannula into the opening. He quickly sealed the hollow tube and moved to repeat the operation on the right carotid. After that, he made a drain incision in the right internal jugular.

Pompey set aside the instrument tray and signed for Sasquatch to bring forward a five-gallon jug of the elixir. The mute then filled two oversized syringes with the greenish yellow fluid and affixed them to the carotid tubes. Then, with Pompey on the left, Sasquatch on the right, the plungers on the syringes were slowly but firmly pushed home, forcing nearly a gallon of elixir re-vitae into the subject's veins. There was a burst of black, oxygen-depleted blood from the dead man's jugular as it was displaced by the invading liquid. The smell that accompanied the expulsion was a familiar one for Mirablis, but unpleasant nonetheless. He coughed thickly and daubed his upper lip with a mixture of lanolin and rose oil in order to better tolerate the stench. He then methodically repeated his drainage procedures on the femoral arteries, draining blood from the right leg while forcing elixir into the left. The old blood collected in the gutters gouged into the table's surface and flowed sluggishly into pails positioned under its drains.

Mirablis walked back to the head of the table, lifting the cadaver's hands to make sure gravity had done its job properly. He paused to marvel over how refined the subject's hands were. Not the sort one would imagine finding on the wrists of a farmer. But there was no point in dwelling on whom or what this man had been. He would be able to tell him all these things himself soon enough—providing he survived the revivification process with his wits and language center intact.

He whistled tunelessly to himself as he exposed the axillary arteries in both the left and right arms. While he was waiting for the last of the blood to drain into metal catch basins, he busied himself with replacing the crow-pecked eye with a new one. Luckily for their friend, one of the elixir's properties was its ability to prevent tissue rejection. And when it came to organ transplants—he could not hope to be in better hands, aged though they were. Even though Mirablis was no longer as young as he once was, he was still capable enough to splice optic nerves. However, he did not feel nearly as confident in regard to the subject's broken neck. From his experiments and observations, he had learned that while the revivification process returned the dead to life and imparted them with a vitality that bordered on the immortal, it had its limit. And damage to the spinal cord and brain after revival seemed to be it. But that decision would have to wait after he'd finished purging the body.

Mirablis moved back and forth, checking and double-checking the limbs, massaging them vigorously to ensure the elixir was spread evenly throughout the emptied veins. It was exceptionally important that the hands and the face were thoroughly saturated; any discoloration in the subject's body and legs could be easily disguised, but the hands and the face were necessary in order for him to pass as normal. Bandages and masks invariably called attention to themselves, and gloves interfered with dexterity. Besides, physical appearance had everything to do with how the subject would be received by the public. Something as grotesque as Sasquatch was good enough for testing out theories and techniques, but it would be of little use in winning the hearts and minds of the hoi polloi.

Mirablis motioned for Pompey to roll the corpse over to one side so he could inject dosages of the elixir re-vitae directly into its buttocks. Without natural circulation to speed the fluid on its way through the body, he had discovered it was better to be safe than sorry. He eyed the corpse's slightly distended belly then thumped it experimentally with his thumb and forefinger before selecting a long, slender trocar and inserting it through the navel. There was a sound similar to that of air escaping from a child's balloon, immediately followed by a strong, foul odor that forced Mirablis to turn away from the work at hand. Once he had recomposed himself, he pumped an infusion of elixir into the abdomen via a large hypodermic.

Satisfied with his handiwork, Mirablis stepped away from the body. Pompey silently moved in and, taking up the needle and thread from the instrument tray, began to suture the veins together again then return them to their rightful places with the exact same care he gave to darning his master's socks.

Mirablis pulled a handkerchief from his pocket to mop his brow as he sat down on a nearby chair. Though he was tired, his energy was still high. He was very excited about the prospects for this subject. In many ways, this was the ideal specimen. He desperately needed this one to succeed; he knew that this was very likely his last chance. He was close to a century in age. He'd outlived virtually everyone he'd ever known, with the exception of Pompey—and Pompey didn't count, really, since he technically died forty years ago.

He could only hope that the new subject did not share the same unfortunate side effects of revivification as Pompey and Sasquatch. And, if he did return to the land of the living, that he could use the tongue in his head to do more than scream. The last three revivals all had to be dismantled because of their unfortunate tendency to do nothing more than shriek and claw at their own flesh—and anything else that moved. To bring back a walking, talking, reasoning white man from beyond the grave was all he needed to finally be able to announce to the world: "This is my gift to you, and it is good!"

Pompey tapped his master on the shoulder, awaking the old man from a doze.

"Ah! Finished already, are we?" Mirablis said, peering at the sutures that ran along the dead man's neck, thighs and inner arms. "Excellent work, Pompey! Excellent! I'll make a surgeon of you yet! You may return him to the tank."

Pompey glanced at the unnatural position of the body's neck then back at Mirablis.

"No, I did not forget, Pompey!" Mirablis said with a dry laugh. "I am not that old a fool! I've decided not to repair the neck surgically and run the risk that the scalpel might slip and damage the spinal cord after the elixir has started its work. I have elected to use a less . . . intrusive . . . means of correcting our friend's neck problem. But all that will have to wait."

As Sasquatch placed the body within its cradle, Pompey stepped forward and fitted a metal skullcap onto its shaven head. An umbilicus of braided copper wire as thick as a man's finger ran from the top of the skullcap and passed through a hole drilled in the lid of the tank, where it lay on the cavern floor in a great coil, like a serpent from ancient myth. At the other end of the umbilicus was a huge lightning rod.

"You know what to do," Mirablis said.

The Indian silently strapped the lightning rod across his back and hefted the heavy coil of copper wiring onto his shoulder.

Then, with barely a grunt, the patchwork shaman began his climb from the bowels of the earth to the vault of heaven.

Chapter Seven

ONE OF THE PRIMARY REASONS Mirablis had chosen this particular cavern to set up shop was that it possessed a natural chimney that permitted the circulation of fresh air from the outer world. As it so happened, the flue that served as the ventilation shaft was wide enough to accommodate a solitary climber. A normal, healthy adult male could make his way to the surface in three hours. Sasquatch, on the other hand, usually reached the top in just under forty-five minutes.

Sasquatch enjoyed climbing the chimney, as it was one of the few times where he was free of the old man. Without Mirablis's stream-of-consciousness monologues filling his mind, Sasquatch's thoughts were finally able to emerge. However, his thoughts were no more his own than were those given to him by Mirablis.

Once, long ago, Sasquatch had been a shaman. A warrior. A maker of shields. A buffalo hunter. But not as one man. Before the pony soldiers came, his name had not been Sasquatch, but Iron Crow. And Small Eagle. And Lean Bear. And Yellow Elk. There were others living within him as well—but these four were the loudest inside his head.

Sasquatch often sat in the darkness of the cave and traced the scars that covered his body, listening to the voices inside him as they counted and cataloged what part belonged to whom.

Lean Bear would always start it off by saying: "The right arm is mine."

Then Small Eagle would chime in with: "The left arm belongs to me!"

"The right leg was once my own," Yellow Elk would reply.

Often the voices got into arguments as to whose body part was the most useful or strongest. Sometimes the discussions would get quite heated. Just when Sasquatch thought that the three would come to blows, Iron Crow would intone in his wisest voice: "But *mine* is his head and *mine* is his heart." This always made the others fall silent, much to Sasquatch's relief.

But try as he might, not even the part of Sasquatch that was Iron Crow could understand Mirablis' drive to conquer Death. A world without Death was a world out of balance—the very essence of madness. Yet, if there was one thing Sasquatch had learned, it was that most white men were crazy.

Over the years Sasquatch had watched Mirablis try time and time again to bring white men back from the spirit world. Those that emerged from the tank had all been worse than crazy, even in the eyes of the whites. They shook and foamed at the mouth like rabid animals while screaming and trying to bite and claw everything around them. Sasquatch believed they came back from the spirit world that way because most white men are a part of nothing but themselves, even when they are made of pieces of other white men. They were simply not used to living together, fighting together and dying together, as his people were.

Or perhaps the reason for their madness was because the white men Mirablis had tried to bring back were men whose bodies were unmourned and buried in paupers' graves. Maybe what they had seen while they were in the spirit world was what made them scream so horribly.

However, Sasquatch had a feeling the hanged man might be different. It was said among his people that the life of a man could be read in the manner of his death. In that case, the hanged man had died trying to protect something that was and yet was not of himself. Sasquatch knew what it was like to die that way.

The giant's train of thought was broken by a strong blast of cold air whistling down the flue. He shrugged the lightning rod off his crooked back and shoved it and what remained of the coil of copper wiring through the crevice that opened onto the surface. He then wriggled out through the narrow opening.

Sasquatch straightened himself as well as his crooked back allowed, blinking the dirt from his eyes. Glancing over the edge of the cliff, he could glimpse the roof of the cabin a hundred feet below. Looking out on the surrounding foothills and the imposing mountains that rose just beyond them, he smiled as a feeling of peace came over him. He muttered a small prayer to the ancestors of his people.

Unlike Pompey, Sasquatch was not truly mute, but the effort it took for him to speak aloud effectively rendered him speechless under normal circumstances. Having finished his prayer, Sasquatch picked up the heavy lightning rod and jammed its sharpened point into the ground, then crouched low on his haunches and opened the leather bag he wore on his breechcloth. He removed from his medicine pouch a pair of thunderstones, marked with the signs known only to shamans and the spirits who serve them. As Sasquatch rattled the bones of the ancient beast-gods in his cupped hands, he began to chant in a voice twisted by disuse.

Even though it was the wrong time of year, and the conditions not right for such weather, storm clouds began to mass in the sky above. Sasquatch's distorted chant grew louder, more like the cry of an animal than a voice lifted in prayer. The clouds became heavier and darker, their bellies sporadically lit from within by brief flashes of purple white light. Sasquatch's chant grew faster and louder, until he was shouting over the howling wind that shook the stunted trees and scrub that surrounded him.

Then, with a final, agonized cry that sent bloody spittle flying from his lips, a burning finger stabbed forth from the storm clouds and struck the lightning rod, followed by an explosion than shook the entire hillside.

Immediately following the thunderclap came a sudden clattering noise, as if a horde of giant warriors were banging their shields with their spears. Hailstones the size of quail eggs began to pour from the sky. Even though the chunks of ice struck with the force of stones from a sling, the nearly naked Sasquatch did not flinch as he knelt to embrace the storm, his jet black hair crackling with static electricity.

Chapter Eight

JOHNNY PEARL NEVER REALLY had a good picture in his mind of what Heaven might look like. To tell the truth, he never really saw much point in worrying over it, since he was pretty sure he wasn't ever going to be let in. Back when he was a boy growing up in North Carolina, the preacher always seemed a lot more interested in warning the congregation about what was waiting for them in Hell than what they had to look forward to in Heaven. Still, Johnny had been under the general impression that Paradise was full of folks dressed in long white gowns with little wings sticking out their backs and halos over their heads, plucking harps and the like.

He wasn't exactly sure where he was, but one thing was certain—it wasn't any Heaven he had heard tell of. But it wasn't any Hell he was familiar with neither. There weren't any mansions in the sky, or angels sitting on clouds, but there sure weren't any fellows with horns and pointy tails poking him in the butt with pitchforks, either.

As far as he could make out, he was at a big barn dance of some sort, with lots of other folk milling around, though he couldn't remember arriving or how he got there. Some of the people who were laughing and talking and dancing looked sort of familiar, though. He could have sworn he saw Abraham Lincoln walk by, strolling alongside Stonewall Jackson. The two sipped cider and chatted like old school chums.

He frowned and turned to study the other guests at the barn dance. Some of the people seemed on their own, while others walked arm in arm or in the company of entire families. Some looked happy, others looked frightened, but the vast majority wore expressions not too different from that of Johnny Pearl's—polite bafflement. As he continued to scan the crowd, he spotted a face in the string band he seemed to know but couldn't place. Then, with a jolt, he recognized the young mandolin player as having been a member of his regiment—one he had personally watch die of a shrapnel wound to the belly. The dead soldier paused long enough to nod hello to his war buddy, then resumed playing.

"*Johnny!*" Someone was calling his name. Someone whose voice he'd thought was stilled forever. "Johnny! Over here!"

Katie waved at him from halfway across the barn, hopping up and down to get his attention. Pearl ran to his wife and snatched her up in his arms, twirling her about so fiercely Katie's feet left the ground.

"I missed you *so* much, Katie!" he said, though he could not remember how long it had been since he last laid eyes on his wife. Had it been weeks? Months? Seconds?

"I missed you too, Johnny." She smiled in return, her gaze fixed on a point just beyond his shoulder. "We *all* did."

He turned to follow the direction of her gaze. Behind him stood his parents and younger brother. They looked exactly as he remembered last seeing them, the day he marched off to join his regiment. He opened his mouth to say how glad he was to see them, how much he had missed them, how sorry he was for not being there when they needed him most, but all that came out was a whispered, "*Mama?*"

Mrs. Pearl held out her hands to her eldest child, her eyes shining with tears of joy. "Oh, Johnny—I knew you'd make it."

He made a soft sobbing noise as he took his mother's hands in his, covering the palms with kisses.

"It's good that you could make it, son," Mr. Pearl said, squeezing his son's shoulder. "We're proud of you, Johnny." His father stepped forward and pulled him into his arms, kissing his cheek as he had the day Johnny went off to war. He was relieved to discover his father still smelled of his favorite pipe tobacco and penny licorice. "Always *have* been, always *will* be."

"Hey, Johnny."

He looked down at his younger brother, forever frozen at ten years old. "Hey, Tommy," he smiled in return, his hand dropping onto the boy's curly head.

Tommy frowned and cocked his head to one side. "How come you look different, Johnny?"

"It's been a long time since you last saw me, Tommy," Pearl explained gently.

"That's okay," Tommy replied, beaming up at his older brother. "Even though you look different, I still knew it was you."

"Come, Johnny," Katie said, holding out her arms to her husband. "Come dance with me."

He smiled as he remembered how they used to dance to keep warm during the long, cold winter nights, their only music Katie's sweet voice lifted in song and the howling of the wind in the eaves. As his arm closed about her waist, he felt something grab hold of his suspenders and yank. He frowned and glanced over his shoulder, but there was no one hovering behind him, trying to cut in. He shrugged and turned back to face his wife, pulling Katie closer. There was a second, stronger tug—but this time it pulled him backward several feet, wrenching him free of his wife's embrace.

"Johnny!"

He threw himself forward, doing his best to fight against whatever it was that was pulling him away. Katie grabbed his outstretched hand and tried to keep him from slipping any further, but it was no use. It felt as if someone was pulling him by the hair at the back of his head. Even though his feet were motionless, he continued to slide backward, like an iron filing dragged by a magnet.

As the other guests turned to stare in amazement, the barn doors flew open with a loud crash, revealing a white void beyond their threshold. There was a sound like a great wind roaring. With one final, mighty tug, Johnny Pearl was yanked off his feet and sent flying into the emptiness.

The last thing he saw as he was sucked into the maelstrom at the heart of nothing was Katie leaning out over the threshold, her hand still outstretched in a vain attempt to stop what was happening.

"*I'll wait for you, Johnny—!*" she called after him. "*No matter what—I'll be waiting!*"

And then the barn doors slammed shut.

Everything was blurry, and his left eye ached as if it had been yanked out of his head and stuck back in again. He coughed fitfully, expelling a lung-full of thick, foul-tasting liquid. Though his eyes rolled in their sockets like greased marbles, he was somehow aware of others standing over him. He tried to follow the ill-defined blobs that bobbed in and out of his impaired field of vision, but it was difficult to move his head. All he could make out was that one of the persons leaning over him was male and seemed to be very old. Suddenly the sound cut in, loud enough to make him wince.

"—neck brace. I repeat—don't try to move your head just yet. Do you understand what I'm saying?" Mirablis froze as the subject opened its mouth to reply. He glanced anxiously at Pompey, who showed him the revolver was ready, just in case.

But instead of screaming and clawing at his own flesh, the hanged man whispered one word—"*Why?*"—then lapsed once more into unconsciousness.

Mirablis grinned and shook his fists in the face of God. "*Yes!*" he shouted. "At long last—I've beaten you at your own game, Jehovah!" Still giddy with triumph, he motioned for his servant to put away the revolver. "I must enter all this into my journals while it is all still fresh in my mind! See that our new friend is made as comfortable as possible, and alert me the moment he begins to show signs of emerging from dormancy!"

As the old man headed down the platform steps, he paused halfway, tapping his lower lip thoughtfully. "It occurs to me that it is time I picked a name for our new friend. He needs to be called *something*, doesn't he? And it is only fitting that *I* name my creation, don't you agree?" His wrinkled brow creased even further, and a mischievous light dawned in his eyes. "Ah! Now I have it! I'll call him—Lynch!"

Chapter Nine

THE DARKNESS FLOWED OVER HIM, pouring in through the openings in his skull to flood his being from the inside out, like ink in a bottle. Then, in the very heart of the darkness there emerged a light—at first dim, then gradually growing in intensity, until I made his eyes swim with tears.

"Excellent!" said a voice from somewhere behind the light. As the candle was moved away, an old man's wrinkled face emerged from the half-world of shadows. "I was afraid the tear duct might have been damaged during the replacement, but that appears not to be the case," the ancient stranger said as he returned the candle to the miner's lamp he wore strapped to his head.

A Negro male with salt and pepper hair loomed suddenly into view. There was something peculiar about the black man's appearance, though he couldn't quite place it at first. Then he realized what it was: The whites of his eyes were glowing.

"Wh-where—?" he whispered hoarsely. His throat ached as if it had been cleaned with a curry comb.

"You needn't worry, Mr. Lynch. You're amongst friends now."

He frowned. "Lynch?"

"Yes. That's your name. Don't you remember?"

Though his mind was a jumble of pictures, voices and places, none of them in order, what the old man claimed didn't sound right to him. But he said nothing. It was easier simply to accept what he was being told than question it. If the old man said his name was Lynch, then that was who he was.

He tried to turn his head to get a better look at his surroundings but met with resistance. Confused, he reached for his collarbone and encountered metal and leather.

The old man read the consternation on his face and patted his hand. "Don't worry, it's merely for . . . cosmetic purposes," he said gently.

"What—what happened?"

The old man's eyes narrowed. "Do you not remember?"

"N-no."

"You've been away for awhile, my dear boy, but now you're back."

"I want to sit up," he said, his tone urgent.

"Very well. Pompey, help Mr. Lynch up." The old man moved aside, watching his patient's movements with the same appraising stare a horse breeder gives a new born colt.

From what Lynch could see, they were in a cave that had been retrofitted for human habitation. Mixed in with the more mundane pieces of furniture, such as a table and chairs, were items of such an arcane nature it was hard to tell if they were medical instruments or art objects. After taking in his surroundings, he turned his body slightly toward the old man.

"Who are you?" he rasped.

"I am Doctor Anton Mirablis, late of the Academy of Sciences, former physician to His Excellency, Napoleon I, and graduate of the University of Vienna—"

"You a sawbones?"

Mirablis winced slightly. "In so many words—yes."

"What's wrong with my neck, Doc?"

In way of a reply, Mirablis picked up a silver-chased hand mirror from the nearby table and held it so that it reflected Lynch's body from the torso on up. The face that looked back at him was his own, yet not

45

his. His head and face were as hairless as those of a newborn babe. There was new scarring about his bright blue left eye—which stood in extreme contrast to the brown eye on his right. The brace that supported his upper neck extended from just below his chin to his shoulders and looked like a cross between a medieval torture device and a corset. After a long moment, Lynch finally turned his gaze back to Mirablis.

"You said I've been away. Where was that?"

"Where no one need ever go again," the old man replied.

It really wasn't that difficult for Lynch to accept the fact that he had died and been brought back to life by this kindly old man with the long white hair and slight European accent. It did bother him, however, that he could not remember much about the life he had lead before his death, even though Dr. Mirablis had assured him that such memory loss—he called it "amnesia"—was not uncommon in connection with electrical shocks.

It had been three days since he had been delivered from the artificial womb of the tank, and Lynch was now able to move about without Pompey being there to make sure he didn't fall. It had taken him a while to grow accustomed to the neck brace—especially how it necessitated that he turn his entire body if he wished to look to either side—but it soon became second nature to him. Mirablis was pleased by how quickly he had adapted to the situation.

Lynch sat in a chair as the old man poked and prodded him and hit his knee with a little toy tomahawk-looking hammer.

Every so often he would mutter to himself and scribble something down in a big leather-bound book on the table.

"How am I doin', Doc?"

"Your progress is most exceptional, my dear boy!" he replied. "Your recovery following revivification is much swifter than those of either Pompey or Sasquatch."

Noticing how Lynch shifted uneasily upon the mention of the patchwork creature's name, Mirablis simply laughed and shook his head. "You should not be afraid of poor Sasquatch!" he chided. "He cannot help being as I have made him. And, in a way, you owe him a debt of gratitude."

"What do you mean?"

"Though I devised the method that brought you back—it was Sasquatch who provided the energy to rekindle your spark of life."

"How can that be?" Lynch frowned, even more baffled than before.

"I, myself, have seen Sasquatch summon the lightning the way a country gentleman might whistle up his hounds. It has proven most advantageous for my work to be able to summon the celestial fire at my whim, rather than waiting for an opportune thunderstorm. It is amazing that such a creature composed of illiterate savages, little removed from their prehistoric ancestors, should hold such awesome power, is it not? But then again—is it any more amazing that the dead rise from their graves? But enough about Sasquatch!" Mirablis produced a small, smooth rock from the pocket of his waistcoat, holding it between his thumb and forefinger. "Do you see this stone, Lynch? In a moment, I'm going to let it drop. I want you to grab it before it strikes the ground while looking straight ahead. Do you understand?"

"Yes, sir," Lynch replied, his gaze automatically fixing on the other man's eyes.

"Very good." To the old man's surprise, no sooner had his fingers loosened their grip on the stone then Lynch's hand snatched it away. Indeed, the movement was so quick, a casual viewer might have thought the younger man had simply grabbed the stone out of his hand.

"Amazing! Truly amazing!" Mirablis said, mopping his wrinkled brow with a handkerchief. "Such reflexes—!"

"It wasn't just reflexes," Lynch said matter-of-factly. "I knew when you were going to drop it."

The doctor lifted an eyebrow. "How so?"

"I looked at your eyes. A split second before you let go, I saw the corner of your eyes tighten and your pupil contract.

That's when I knew to make my move."

Mirablis stopped daubing his brow. "Most extraordinary. How did you *know* to look for these signs, dear boy?"

Lynch shrugged as best he could while wearing a neck brace. "I just did. Do you think it's something I learned back when I was alive the first time, Doc?"

"It's possible," Mirablis said absently. The old man took Lynch's hands and opened them, staring at the palms as if they held some mystery within their lines. "But I did not expect such an instinctual response from a man of your background . . . ."

"Background?"

"You were a settler . . . a farmer," Mirablis said cautiously. "You were killed by Indians. Do you remember?"

There was a faraway look in Lynch's brown eye, while the blue remained disturbingly clear. "I remember a cabin. And something about Injuns. But everything else is foggy."

"You memory might come back, or it might not return at all. But in case you do not reclaim your lost memories—do not dwell overmuch on it, my friend. In many ways, the life that was once yours is no more an integral part of your new existence than a cocoon is to the butterfly.

"You are of a new breed—*Homo Mirablis*. I hope you don't think me too forward for naming your species after myself. You are stronger now, possessed of a stamina beyond that of mortal men. You can withstand incredible physical stress and trauma without registering a moment's pain. You need little more than an hour's sleep a day, and to eat only once or twice a month. Your eyesight is as sharp as that of a cat. No matter if it is the dead of winter or the height of summer, weather means nothing to your physical comfort. Disease, old age, infirmity . . . these things no longer hold meaning for you. You are free to pursue all your dreams, all your ambitions without fear or distraction."

"That all sounds mighty nice, Doc. But what are the drawbacks?"

"Drawbacks?" Mirablis shifted uncomfortably. "What do you mean?"

"Well—everything's got two sides, Doc."

Mirablis's cheeks flamed red. "You are speaking nonsense! There is no drawback to immortality! I am very tired now and need to rest." He turned and hurried back to his aboveground quarters with the jerky movements of a man trying to contain his anger.

Lynch could not understand what he did to upset Doc Mirablis. He certainly had not intended to do such a thing. So far the old gentleman had shown him nothing but kindness. It made him feel bad to think he had done something to agitate him in such a way.

He returned to the narrow camp cot that served as his bed and sat down on its far edge, staring at the stalagmites in the cave. He felt as he had when his father used to punish him for whispering in church; except he could not remember what his father's face looked like, or what his name was.

The sound of a foot scraping the ground nearby startled him from his reverie. He glanced up and saw Sasquatch hovering in the shadows, the whites of his eyes glowing eerily in the gloom of the cavern. Lynch suppressed his natural urge to shout in fear and instead met the creature's lambent gaze.

"What do you want?"

The crooked giant took a tentative step forward, eyes burning like twin suns. "She says she still waits for you."

Lynch was not sure what surprised him more: that the creature's voice was like that of rocks being ground together, or that Sasquatch had spoken Cheyenne—and he had understood him perfectly.

Chapter Ten

WHEN MIRABLIS NEXT CAME to see Lynch, the old man wore a contrite expression on his face. "I have been thinking about what you said the other day. You are right. It is only fair that you understand—*truly* understand—the reasons for what I do and what I have done. It is important to me that you comprehend the scope of my experiments and discoveries, so that you may help me in my work, in your own unique way, as Pompey and Sasquatch do in theirs.

"In order to do this, my dear Lynch, I must tell you my story. It begins in a different world, indeed, a different century, than the one we inhabit now. Do you know that I was not brought into this world as Anton Mirablis? My true name is of no importance, really. I cast aside my old identity when I fled Europe for this wondrous country of yours. A new life is deserving of a new name, don't you agree?

"Still, for all of America's raw-boned lawlessness, it is nothing compared to the chaos and madness of the Terror and the wars that followed. This was the world of my youth. I was a gifted child, showing a natural aptitude for the physical sciences early in life. My parents were among those who benefited from the fall of the ancient regime and therefore could afford to indulge my precocious nature.

50

"I was little more than a boy when I was shipped off to the university in Vienna to study medicine. It was there I gained the attention of a brilliant anatomist of the name Viktor von Frankenstein . . . perhaps you have heard of him?"

Lynch frowned and squinted. "The name sounds familiar—but I can't remember nothin' about it except that it's from a made-up story."

"Oh, Viktor was real enough, I assure you! Just as Kit Carson and Wild Bill Hickok and Buffalo Bill are real. And the story told about my old friend and colleague was just as far removed from the truth as the tales about their exploits.

"I soon learned that Viktor and I shared similar interests—mainly a desire to break Death's grip on the mind of man. He needed someone to help him with his research, but he did not want a mere assistant—he required someone as intelligent and as dedicated as himself. He needed someone who could be trusted to understand the problems such unorthodox experiments faced, someone willing to brave the dangers they held, both physically and socially. And, to his credit, he was capable of recognizing those qualities in me despite my tender years.

"Ours was a close and, by default, secretive relationship. The intensity of our shared obsession, at times, bound us more tightly than lovers. We worked side by side, in an atmosphere of such emotional intensity that it was bound that we would eventually have a serious falling out. What caused our disagreement was a divergence between us on how best to realize our goal. Viktor was convinced that a body stitched together from the undamaged pieces of cadavers could be given life through applying electrical current to the nervous system. However, I was concerned with the question of decay, which led to my creation of the elixir re-vitae as a means of restoring and preserving soft tissues.

"Essentially, our differences lay in our own very personal interpretations of the act of Creation. For Viktor, it was all very Promethean and Old Testament, with lightning and fire from Heaven and the like. He would fashion himself a man of clay and breathe the fire of Life into it and that was that. I, on the other hand, looked not to mythology, but man himself—or should I say, woman?—for my inspiration.

Dissecting the cadavers of pregnant women revealed to me that we are creatures of the sea, and that within every female there is a secret ocean, in which the evolution of our species is re-enacted, from briny shrimp to naked ape.

"In the end, though Viktor was my elder, it was he who suffered the problem most associated with youth—impatience. He wanted results. My method was far too slow to suit his tastes. In any case, there was a serious falling out between us, which resulted in us going our separate ways.

"I made the best of my situation by attaching myself to Napoleon's personal entourage, eventually becoming one of the physicians in charge of the battlefield hospitals. This gave me unprecedented—and unsupervised—access to all the amputated limbs I could ever want. However, when I traveled with him to Egypt, my interest was piqued by rumors of certain recipes and formulae concerning the preservation and resurrection of the dead found in a scroll believed to be written by the lord high embalmer to the pharaohs.

"However, not long after my return to Europe from the mysterious Orient, I received a package containing the journals and notes of my former friend and colleague. Along with these was a letter from Viktor, informing me that he had been forced to abandon his experiments. He conceded my method of reviving the dead was superior to his own—though he warned me of dire consequences should I pursue my interests.

"As I read his journals, I learned that Viktor did, indeed, build a man from the bodies of the dead. He succeeded in bringing it back to life using the harnessed power of a thunderstorm. That much of the story is true. However, the creature that rose from that slab was no more capable of narrating its own plight than it could fly to the moon. The thing was . . . damaged in the brain.

And, to make matters worse, not long after it was revived, it began to rot. To spend so many years and so much energy on research, and to have nothing to show for it but a wretched, stinking imbecile! It was all too much for Viktor, I'm afraid.

"However, when the rumors concerning Viktor's connection to the creature that had slain not only him, but at least six other people, began to circulate, I deemed it wise to remove myself from the Continent. That is when I came to this country. I first arrived in Philadelphia, where I quickly established myself under my new name . . . that of Dr. Anton Mirablis. For several years, I was able to pursue my experiments in relative secret, with able assistance from Pompey, who I purchased from the master who abused him so cruelly.

"It was during these years that I attempted to refine the elixir revitae, combining it with the ancient Egyptian formulae. It was very difficult to locate the necessary elements needed for the mixture, and the slightest variation in temperature during the distilling could have proven disastrous. It was a long process of trial and error, but eventually I succeeded in keeping amputated limbs and other organs from not only rotting, but continuing their original functions as well. Yet, try as I might, I was unable to generate the necessary spark of life that Viktor had managed to infuse in his creation, hapless as it may have been.

"I eventually came to the decision that what was needed for me to succeed was to combine my technique with that of Viktor's. So I set about creating a giant womb, if you will, and filling it with elixir, whose special properties would be activated by passing massive electric currents through both it and the subject. Are you ready for some fresh air—?"

"Sure," Lynch said, taken aback by the suddenness of Mirablis's suggestion.

"Very good. I'll use the occasion to introduce you to the subject of my first successful revival."

After the darkness of the cavern, the pale light of a winter day was enough to make Lynch's eyes water. He stood for a moment in front of the cabin and stared at his surroundings, hoping to summon forth a memory that might tell him who he was.

"So—where's this fella you brought back from the dead, Doc?" he said, glancing over at Mirablis, who was bundled in a buffalo-skin coat and a hat made from a rabbit.

"He's over here, my boy," he said, gesturing toward a small barnlike structure built alongside the cabin.

The interior of the stable was dark and close, with most of the space occupied by a medicine wagon. Standing in the solitary stall was a coal black stallion, nosing a mound of straw. In the dim light, it looked as if the beast's eye sockets were filled with smoldering fire.

Lynch turned to fix Mirablis with a stare of utter disbelief. "*A horse—?!?*"

The old man shrugged. "It was a matter of convenience. I needed to test my technique on something large—and it was far easier to get my hands on a livery animal than a baboon or gorilla. I suppose I *could* have used a pig, but their flesh spoils so quickly . . . ."

Mirablis shuffled forward, smiling indulgently at the beast as it pawed the ground. "Do you know anything about mythology?"

"I can't rightly say," Lynch said, shrugging his shoulders. "I remember something about a guy with thunderbolts—and something about a fella with wings on his feet and a pie plate on his head."

"It doesn't really matter," Mirablis replied. "Viktor used to joke about how he was Prometheus while I was Pluto. Prophetic, don't you think, considering where I have ended up—and how he ended? Still, that is why I chose to name this fine animal after the horse that pulled the chariot of the Lord of the Underworld: Alastor.

"In any case, as of June 27th, 1840, he became the first successful subject of my revivification process, and he has served me most ably ever since." Mirablis's hand dipped into his coat pocket and produced gobbets of raw meat. To Lynch's surprise, the horse eagerly gobbled them down as it they were lumps of sugar.

"That's a good boy," Mirablis smiled, stroking the beast's neck.

"Y-you just fed that animal meat!"

Mirablis's smile disappeared instantly. "It is cold out here. Let's go back inside. I felt the need for some hot tea."

Pompey hurried forward and helped the old man out of his burdensome coat and hat as they entered the cabin. The old man hobbled to the table, where a white porcelain tea pot sat, along with a solitary matching cup. Mirablis motioned for Lynch to take the seat opposite him at the table.

"You asked me the other day about the . . . side effects that accompany revivification. I will admit that I was . . . unprepared for such a question, and I responded most rudely. But you are right—if anyone deserves straight answers as to what to expect, it is you.

"When I killed Alastor the first time, he was a three-year-old stallion at the height of his stamina. In the decades that have passed since, he has not aged a day, nor has he ever been ill. He can ride for days on end without rest or food and still remain as strong as a dozen horses. Yet there have been—changes in his nature. Such as the one you saw. Alastor is no longer a harmless herbivore, like others of his kind. He now has a taste for flesh. However, he only needs to be fed once every six weeks . . . not unlike certain large snakes."

"But he's just a *horse*," Lynch said anxiously. "That doesn't mean those changes will occur in a *human*—right?"

Mirablis sighed as he lifted his tea cup. "There is much even *I* don't understand about the revivification process, I'm afraid. *Why* is there heightened strength? *Why* is there a reduction in the need for sleep and a suppression of appetite? And, most important of all, *why* can't the subjects digest anything but raw meat?"

"You mean I'm some kinda *ghoul*?" Lynch shouted, his voice cracking as he jumped to his feet. Pompey stepped forward and pointed a pistol directly at his head.

"Pompey! Put that away!" Mirablis snapped. "There's no need for it! Our friend is merely upset—and justifiably so! Please, Lynch—sit back down. You're making Pompey nervous."

Lynch sat down slowly while keeping an eye on the mute. Pompey, for his part, did not lower the gun until Lynch was once again seated.

Mirablis clucked his tongue in reproof. "You're agitating yourself for no reason, my boy! As I said, feeding occurs only once every six weeks, and is easily controlled, if you prepare for it properly. A couple of bighorn sheep is usually enough to keep Pompey and Sasquatch satisfied. Just because you *must* eat raw flesh in order to survive does not make you a monster! Besides, your diet is the least of your problems. One major drawback to your new life is that you must pay a great deal of attention to your physical integrity. Since your pain threshold is so incredibly high, it tends to block signals regarding "minor" injuries. What this means is you are in constant danger of accidentally losing a body part without being aware of it. Fingers and toes are the most vulnerable, as well as the ears. However, it's nothing a little needle and thread can't fix.

"You will need to undergo periodic checks for signs of corruption . . . since its likely not all portions of your body were infused with equal amounts of the elixir re-vitae. Those areas that may have been missed will gradually begin to rot, if not caught in time. I'll show you the proper means of administering injections to yourself later on. Should access to the elixir revitae prove difficult, soaking your body in cold water is a suitable stopgap."

"That's all well and good, Doc—but you still haven't told me how you ended up living in a cave with Pompey and Sasquatch for company."

Mirablis blinked. "No, I haven't, have I? I'm afraid I'm easily distracted nowadays. Thank you for reminding, my dear boy. Now, where was I—? Well, you can imagine how pleased I was by how Alastor turned out. Then, less than a week later, I was presented with a chance to try my process on a *human* subject! I was holding a dinner party for some of my fellows at the Academy. While I despise such charades, I've long accepted the necessity of maintaining the proper respectability, especially in a city such as Philadelphia.

"However, much to my chagrin, Pompey suffered a massive heart attack and died while in the middle of serving the poached trout! Of course, it was simply 'not done' to cancel a dinner party because a servant—a slave, at that—had keeled over dead during the main course. Imagine, if you can, my consternation as I was forced to endure several more hours of meaningless chit-chat with those empty-headed boobies, all the while knowing that Pompey's body was succumbing to decomposition! After the evening sherry and cigars were done with, I lost no time in hurrying my tiresome 'fellow intellectuals' out of the house.

"It took hours for me to prepare Pompey's body for revivification, using a variation on the voltaic cell developed by John Daniell to force a sufficient electrical charge through Pompey's body, thereby activating the elixir and reviving him. He was just as he was before—save he no longer could speak. I was delighted to have my faithful assistant returned to me, but I was frustrated by Pompey's inability to express his experiences and physical symptoms to me, except in dumb show. And since he had never learned how to read and write—after all, teaching slaves such things was sorely frowned on in those days—I was at something of a loss. Then there was the question of how to explain Pompey's return after he had died very publicly, in front of my so-called peers, without alerting them to what I was doing?

"Since I did not feel my work was ready for such scrutiny, I decided to leave Philadelphia and pursue my research elsewhere. For several years I wandered the country, keeping households everywhere from New Orleans to Minneapolis—all the while attempting to replicate my success with Pompey, but with disappointing results.

"I discovered there was still much to learn—as Pompey and Alastor soon showed me. Little over a month after his revivification, Alastor went berserk in New Orleans and kicked down his stall—assaulting and devouring his stable mate. Not long after that happened, Pompey ate three servants in my employ. Luckily, they were slaves, so their disappearance did not raise any alarms. Believe me; Pompey was most contrite about what happened. And except for occasional lapses into frenzy—not unlike those of a woman enslaved to the cycle of the moon—he has remained as sober as a judge. Once I began to understand the nature of his attacks, I was able to prepare in advance, thus making sure Pompey received nourishment without killing anything more sentient than a steer.

"When the War Between the States erupted, I knew neither North nor South would be safe for me—so I opted to head West.

I assumed the guise of a medicine-show drummer, which allowed me to continue my experiments—and for a nickel, Pompey would bite the head off any animal the audience cared to provide, which helped cut down on expenses, as you might expect.

"I used the medicine show to test various weakened and recombined formulas of the elixir re-vitae designed specifically for oral consumption, and discovered that while it could not cure the croup or the Regrets of Venus, it *did* seem to have an effect on cancer. Then, eight years ago, I came across the remains of an Indian camp.

"There had been a recent massacre of unspeakable barbarity. Not only the braves, but the women and children—even the elders of the tribe—had been systematically butchered. I was lucky in that the massacre sight was relatively fresh and had yet to be scavenged by crows and coyotes. I harvested the least damaged body parts and proceeded to make myself a composite human, just as Viktor had done.

"I will admit that my motives were a combination of scientific curiosity and pride. I was determined to stitch together a human that would be an improvement over Viktor's infamous monster. The result was Sasquatch.

"There is no doubt in my mind that he is superior to Viktor's poor mad, rotting creature. However, Sasquatch was basted together from bodies that were far from . . . fresh, which may account for the difficulty he has with speaking. Another problem is that compared to Pompey, Sasquatch is noticeably . . . awkward, though astonishingly strong. Still, aesthetically speaking, he is far from pleasing. That is where you come in, my handsome lad."

"Handsome—?" Lynch snorted derisively. "You're calling *me* handsome?"

"In comparison to that which has gone before, you are Michelangelo's David!" Mirablis said with a flourish of his hand. "Granted, the neck brace is far from fashionable, and your eyes don't match—but you are otherwise presentable. Most importantly, my boy, you are *white*. What good would it do me to show the Academy a redskin I've brought back from the dead—? After all, they're doing their damnedest to wipe them off the face of the planet!

"More importantly—I need you to serve as heir to my work. You have demonstrated the intelligence and dexterity necessary to be trained in the techniques of reviving the dead. With my knowledge and your innate skill, mankind need never be inconvenienced by mortality ever again! Think of it, Lynch—just *think!*"

"Yeah—I'm thinkin'," Lynch muttered. "Look, Doc—I realize you did all this to help folks out, just like that fella that invented laudanum or Mr. Fulton and his steam engine. But did it ever occur to you even *once* while you was doin' all this—that mebbe there's better things than simply being alive . . . and worse things than being dead?"

Mirablis frowned and cocked his head to one side. "Interesting. I wonder if you were as prone to philosophy before your death. Pompey, return our new friend to the cave."

The mute stepped forward and motioned with the muzzle of his gun for Lynch to rise.

Chapter Eleven

THAT NIGHT SHE CAME TO HIM, emerging from the shadows of the cave as if she had always dwelt within them. She was lit from within by a pale fire that burned like a swarm of fireflies trapped in a jar.

"Hey, Johnny."

Even though Lynch did not know his first name, upon hearing it on her lips, he knew it to be his. "Hello," he replied.

"Do you remember me?" she asked.

"Yes, I remember you," he said, his voice shaking.

"I still wait," she whispered, and, having said that, she disappeared like a candle flame snuffed between wetted fingers.

Lynch lowered his head into his hands and stared at his feet. He remembered it all now: his family, the war, his life as an outlaw . . . and Katie. And he remembered how all those things had been lost to him, and then found—only to be torn away from him a second, horrible time. He looked up to find the twisted visage of Sasquatch peering down at him. To his surprise, the patchwork creature no longer frightened him.

"How can you serve him?" Lynch asked the giant, speaking in his native tongue.

Sasquatch shrugged his uneven shoulders. "Mirablis repaired me the best way he knew how. And now my tribe, though dead, lives within me still. In my own fashion, I am content, my brother."

"Why did you show her to me? It was you who did that, wasn't it?"

"I did it so that you would not forget. You were a man of honor, Johnny Pearl—and that sense of honor lives within you still."

"How did you know that was my name—?"

"There are no secrets for those who speak with the dead," Sasquatch said. "I saw it as my duty to awake your memories, since the old man was unwilling to do so. He is afraid you will insist on hunting down those who killed you and your squaw, if you knew the truth."

"Then he was right to be afraid—because that's *exactly* what I intend to do!"

Sasquatch nodded his head sagely. "I will show you how to escape this place, if that is what you want."

"Escape—? You mean I'm being held prisoner?"

The giant fixed him with a dubious look. "Do you feel you are free to leave this place whenever you like?"

"Good point," Lynch grunted. "So—what do you propose? Wait until the old man's asleep and then sneak out the door?"

Sasquatch shook his head. "Mirablis is no real concern—the problem is Pompey. He is loyal to his master without question. And he does not sleep. He stands guard over the old man while he slumbers, effectively blocking the way through the cabin."

"So what are you telling me—that I'll have to kill Pompey to get out of here?"

Sasquatch shook his head. "No, there is another way out—one that not even Pompey knows of."

The giant stood up and motioned for Lynch to follow, leading him into one of the smaller tunnels that branched off from the main cavern. The tunnel quickly narrowed so that they had to turn sideways in order to squeeze through. Suddenly the passage widened again, ending in a cul-de-sac. Sasquatch shot Lynch a conspiratorial smile over his shoulder as he reached out and moved a chunk of the wall, an impossible feat for anyone not possessing the strength of the resurrected. There was a sudden gust of chill air and a spill of dim light that—in comparison to the gloom of the cave—seemed as bright as the heart of the sun. Along with the burst of cold and sunlight came the odor of manure and straw.

Alastor did not seem at all surprised to see Sasquatch and Lynch emerge from the wall. The stallion snorted and tossed its head, pawing the floor of its stall. Sasquatch smiled with his crooked mouth and stroked the beast's raven black neck.

"This animal has a great heart. He will take you where you must go without complaint or fear."

Lynch opened the barn door and glanced outside. The wind was blowing a mixture of sleet and snow down from the mountains. "There's a storm coming."

"That is why you must hurry. If you wait much longer, it will be impossible to leave before the spring."

"But I can't leave now! I'm not dressed for it! I don't have any provisions—"

"Have you eaten since you emerged from the tank?"

"No," he admitted.

"Then what need have you for provisions? And as for your clothes," Sasquatch gestured to the buckskins and woolen shirt Lynch was wearing, "you will find you are dressed warmly enough."

"Are you *mad*—? My blood will freeze in my veins!"

Sasquatch smiled crookedly. "*Blood*? You have no blood." Sasquatch held up his left hand and sliced open the palm with the knife that hung from his belt. A greenish yellow fluid welled from the wound, like sap from a sugar maple. "The cold is nothing to our kind, little brother." He reached behind a bale of hay and produced a laden saddlebag, which he tossed to Lynch. "All you need is in that bag: flasks of elixir re-vitae, a syringe, and some needle and thread. Use it wisely."

Alastor fixed Lynch with a curious stare but did not resist the bit placed between his teeth or the saddle cinched about his belly. There was a self-awareness to the beast, born from living decades beyond its natural span that Lynch found almost human.

As he swung himself into the saddle, he found himself eye to eye with the patchwork giant. Lynch felt a flush of shame as he remembered how he had first reacted to the Indian's appearance. "I cannot thank you enough for what you have done for me, Sasquatch."

"The part of me who helped you is called Iron Crow."

"Then I thank that which is Iron Crow," Lynch replied. "But still—I don't understand. Why do you stay here, if is so easy for you to leave? Why do you serve Mirablis as you do?"

"I attend the white man out of respect for his knowledge, for he is indeed wise. But he is also mad. He made me, and in his way he is both my father and my mother—as such, I owe him my life and my loyalty. And I know, for as much as he desires to free mankind from Death, he fears the process he has created. When he dies—his knowledge dies with him. So I stay with him—to make sure it does." The giant suddenly shook his head, as if trying to dislodge something from his ear. "Enough talk! Iron Crow says you must leave now or not at all! Go—! And good hunting to you, Lynch-who-once-was-Johnny-Pearl."

Lynch put his heels to Alastor's flanks. The horse took flight, nimbly making its way down the twisting path that lead to the cabin. As they made their way down the side of the mountain, he looked back, but there was nothing to see except a jumble of scrub and rock.

Chapter Twelve

THE WINDS HOWLED DOWN out of the mountains and across the high plains like damned souls loosed from the coldest regions of Hell, tearing at the flesh and clothes of the solitary rider making his away across the forbidding steppes. Yet, despite a naked scalp covered by a gleaming skullcap of frost and buckskins so stiff with ice they creaked, the lone horseman showed no sign of discomfort. Nor did his mount slow its relentless pace as it made its way through the stinging sleet and snow, even when it was forced to shoulder its way through drifts as tall as a man.

All that was left was the chimney.

Once, not that long ago, Johnny Pearl and Katie Small Dove had danced before its fire, made love before its warmth. Now it jutted from the jumble of charred timber like a skeletal finger, pointing at the bleak winter sky. If it had not remained standing, Lynch would have ridden past without realizing it, since what few landmarks that existed were otherwise shrouded in snow and ice.

Once he spotted it, he used the landmark to triangulate the location of the stand of cottonwood trees. When he found the one they had used to hang him, he stood for a moment, staring up at the six-inch length of frayed rope still flapping from the branch.

It took him somewhat longer to find what was left of Katie's body. As he swept the snow away from her, he was struck by how perfectly preserved she appeared to be—like one of those ice princesses in the fairy tales his mama used to read to him as a child. She was lying on her side, much like the last time he remembered seeing her before he died. The scavengers hadn't done much to the carcass, possibly because she froze to the ground quickly, which made the mutilations done to her appear even more bestial.

It took Lynch two days to build the cairn using the natural stone from the chimney. He used a rusty shovel he found amid the ruins of the shed and, summoning the fearsome strength that was his new birthright, single-handedly demolished the fireplace.

He worked day and night without respite, oblivious to the damage he was doing to himself. When the blisters burst, a yellowish green ichor streamed forth across his palms instead of blood.

Once he had built the cairn over his wife's body, Lynch turned his attention to the flagstone that ringed the hearth. When the shovel's blade shattered, he tossed it aside and continued digging at the frozen ground with his bare hands until he succeeded in finally unearthing a package wrapped in oil cloth, inside of which was a bundle of neatly folded black clothes and a pearl-handled revolver.

He lifted the killing piece and pressed the length of its cold muzzle against his cheek, stroking his face with it as if it were made of the finest silk.

I knew you would not forsake me, whispered the gun.

Lynch closed his eyes and said nothing. The dying man crawled on his hands and knees, dragging a lap of gut in his wake. The dying man's name was Polk and, up until an hour ago, he'd been out on a toot with a couple of his desperado buddies in some piss-ant cow town.

Polk knew O'Donoghue and Wagner from when they used to ride with Drake. But, unlike them, Polk did not consider himself a gunslinger. And since someone had been making a point of going after men from Drake's regiment the last few months, he was quick to remind folks that he was just a scout who kept colorful company, nothing more. O'Donoghue was of the opinion the killings were done by vigilantes who'd gotten brave now that Drake was officially declared a renegade Back East. It wasn't surprising, given the red-headed bastard's proclivities.

Wagner and O'Donoghue had deserted a while back, but whoever was gunning for Drake probably wasn't one for splitting hairs. It was Wagner's idea that they hit the saloon as a team, just to be on the safe side Wagner had said there was safety in numbers, and this way they could drink, gamble and whore while watching one another's backs, which had made sense to Polk at the time.

But that was before the man in black showed up.

Polk had figured the stranger for trouble when he first entered the saloon. He was tall, dressed in a tattered black duster that had blotches of graveyard mold on the sleeves. He wore a pearl-handled revolver low on his hip. The stranger walked real stiff, like that steam-operated mechanical man Polk saw at the circus once. But the strangest thing about the man in black was his eyes—they didn't match.

The stranger walked right up to their table and opened fire without so much as a "howdy doo." Wagner and O'Donoghue were dead before they could put down their cards—and Polk would have met the exact same fate if that fancy pearl-handled gun hadn't misfired.

He didn't know what the stranger's quarrel was with Wagner and O'Donoghue, and he wasn't about to waste time asking. Polk jumped to his feet and fired point-blank into the other man's chest. The man in black staggered but did not go down.

As he tried to flee past the man he'd just shot, the stranger lashed out with a knife, catching him across the gut. Polk had been so frightened that he was on his horse and a mile out of town before he realized the seriousness of his wound. Once the adrenaline wore off, the pain took over, and he looked down to see his lower intestine hanging out of his belly. He fell off his horse not long after that.

Still, even though he was in more pain than he'd ever know again—Polk continued to crawl. Some long-buried sixth sense told him that he had not escaped the man who had tried to kill him. Indeed, it was as if the stranger's mismatched eyes were staring down at him from a great height, watching as he dragged his guts behind him like the losing cur in a dog fight.

It wasn't until he heard the stranger's horse whinny that Polk realized he was lying on his back like a tipped turtle, staring up at a dark figure framed against the hard blue sky.

Lynch carefully dismounted and knelt beside Polk without looking down. As he leaned across the dying man to relieve him of his weapons, Polk glimpsed a metal and leather neck brace underneath the long woolen muffler wrapped around the stranger's throat.

"Where the hell do you think you're runnin' to, you damn fool idjit—?" Lynch snarled. "You think Drake can protect you?"

"Fuck Drake!" Polk spat. "Mister—I don't know what you're talkin' about or why you come after me like you did—I ain't never done nothin' to you—!"

"Like fuck you're innocent!" Lynch growled. "I know you got it on you—that drinkin' buddy of yours in Caspar said so. So where is it?"

"Where's what—?!?" Polk moaned, licking his lips. He was so thirsty he could almost forget the pain in his belly. "Please, Mister . . . I'll be more than happy to tell you whatever it is you want to hear, if you just gimme a drink of water . . . I need a drink real bad . . . ."

Lynch snorted in disgust and began to search the dying man's pockets. As his fingers closed on what lay coiled in Polk's breast pocket, he gave voice to a groan as pained as Polk's own. He lurched stiffly to his feet, pulling the braid from its hiding place like a conjurer producing a scarf.

Lynch ran Katie's hair between his fingers, marveling over how the months since her death had done nothing to diminish its luster or texture. Lynch closed his eyes as he stroked the braid against his cheek. It even smelled of her. The only thing different from when it was still on her head was that Polk had bound the end that had attached to the scalp with a piece of rawhide, so it would not unravel.

"Mister . . ." Polk rasped. "Please . . . I gotta have some water."

Lynch pocketed the length of hair and turned to remove the canteen from his saddle horn. Alastor pawed the ground, tossing his ebony mane.

"I don't like how your hoss is lookin' at me," Polk said.

"What you gonna do about it?" Lynch said, throwing the canteen on the ground. "You know—drinkin' with a belly wound will kill you," he commented laconically as he watched Polk eagerly slurp down the water.

"What do I care—I'm dyin' anyway, ain't I?" rasped Polk, wiping his lips with a trembling hand.

"Reckon so," Lynch replied, studying the length of intestine hanging out of Polk. It oozed blood and less identifiable matter, and had little pieces of gravel stuck to it. It looked bad and smelled worse.

"Tell me one thing before I die, mister," Polk whispered. "Why'd you come gunnin' for me? It weren't just for some squaw braid, was it?"

"You don't recognize me," Lynch sighed. "I don't blame you for that, really. I reckon you never expected to see me again—so why bother committin' th' face to memory?"

Polk squinted at his killer with rapidly failing eyesight. "Hold on . . . *now* I remember you . . . You're that squaw man that was squattin' on Myerling's old homestead. But—I saw you *hang.*"

"Lynched, to be exact."

"That ain't possible!" Polk shook his head, trying to fight the swell of fear rising within him. Dying was one thing, but talking to a man he knew to be dead was another. "You *can't* be him!"

"But I am. Or at least I *was.* I ain't exactly the man I used t'be—but then, who amongst us is? Don't worry, you haven't gone crazy. You remembered correctly. You did see me hang. Just as I saw you desecrate my wife's body. I made a promise over her grave that I would hunt you down, you son of a bitch, and take back what you took from her. I've got her braid—now tell me what you did with the baby."

"B-baby?" The fear in Polk's eyes was replaced by bafflement. "W-what baby?"

"Don't play dumb!" Lynch growled through gritted teeth. "Tell me what you did with the child she was carryin'!"

"I swear as I'm dyin', mister—I took your woman's scalp, but I didn't touch nothin' else on her! What kind of man do you take me for—?!?"

Lynch stared down at the dying man and shook his head. Without saying anything else, he turned his back on Polk and removed the bit from Alastor's mouth. He patted the beast's velvety black neck, and then motioned to the mortally wounded human sprawled on the ground. Alastor tossed his mane in excitement.

Polk struggled to lift his head, squinting up at the dark blur looming over him. "Mister—is that you?"

He only managed to scream once before the horse sank its teeth into his Adam's apple.

Chapter Thirteen

ANTIOCH DRAKE RULED ALL HE SURVEYED.

This meant, at that particular moment, he was the lord and master of twelve houses, a general store, a livery barn, a church, a saloon, nineteen men, twenty-three women and twelve children—not counting the ones he'd left lying dead in the street.

It was the third day of Drake's reign over what once had been the frontier settlement of Newtonville. Now, after seventy-two hours of near-continuous rapine, it bore a closer resemblance to Hell than anywhere else.

During the fifteen years he'd spent dealing with Indians, Drake had become an expert on overcoming small communities of civilians. The techniques he had used to place Newtonville under his control were no different from those he once utilized against Cheyenne and Sioux villages: He came in fast and early, striking while his opponents were still in their beds.

While Drake no longer had a battalion at his command, those who remained loyal and followed him into the wilderness were more than a match for sleepy-eyed settlers in their long johns. His first order was the systematic slaughter of all males young enough and healthy enough to prove troublesome. Their bodies now lay side by side in the street as both a warning and reminder to the others as to what to expect should they step out of line.

His second order was the culling of those women who could pass muster as whores. The third order was to lock up all those who remained in the town church—mostly older men, grannies, and young'uns—until he was ready to give his fourth and final order. And when that order came—it would be heard as far away as Washington.

He had been betrayed by his government—and now he was going to make his former employer pay by taking out his revenge on the people it held so dear. For fifteen years, Washington had turned a blind eye to how he handled the "Indian problem." Hell, he had even been given medals and commendations for treating Cheyenne camps the exact same way he was handling Newtonville. Drake knew what his role was in the Manifest Destiny of his country: Exterminator. It was his job to see that all the pesky, potentially dangerous vermin that infested the plains would not interfere with the settlement of the Wyoming and Montana territories, or the conversion of the buffalo hunting grounds into cattle ranches. And he had been very good at his job. Very good indeed.

But now his rank, his medals, his career had been stripped away from him, just as vultures tear at the flesh of a fallen lion. And for what? All because some whey-faced city slicker Back East decided he didn't like how Drake was handling the relocation of Injuns to the reservations—as if what had happened at Little Big Horn wasn't proof enough that the red-skinned devils were dangerous savages.

So what if he burned down a few farmhouses and lynched some settlers along the way? This was a war! There could be no middle ground for those who were sympathetic to the enemy—or refused to take sides. And no matter how they might deny it, there was no trusting half-breeds, either—their red blood would always turn against the white. It was a scientific fact. Better to eradicate them entirely than to suffer the indignity of betrayal later on.

When the dispatch came, ordering his return to Washington to answer questions concerning his actions, Drake knew what he had to do. That night he called on those who were loyal to follow him—and rode off with close to twenty men at his side. Thus began the legend of Drake's Devils.

That was six months ago. He had less than half that number still riding with him. Some had deserted, some had died in action, others he'd killed himself. Still, as brigand gangs go, his had proven extremely successful in eluding capture. For all their bluster about being ready to apply for statehood, the Wyoming territory was an isolated, thinly populated place. It was easy for even a larger number of men to evade the authorities—especially if they were lead by someone who knew all their pursuers' tactics by heart. Unless the territorial governor was willing to bring in Texas Rangers to deal with the problem,

Drake and his Devils were free to plunder the countryside with impunity. Drake glanced out the window of his new house. A week ago, it had belonged to the mayor of Newtonville. But Drake had commandeered it solely because he wanted an unobstructed view of the church across the street. He wanted to make sure the guards didn't slack off and let any of the captives escape. Ferguson and Powell were seated on the wooden steps leading to the doors of the church, smoking hand-rolled cigarettes. Each man had a loaded shotgun resting across his knees. The moment the front door of Drake's house opened, they snapped to attention. Drake stalked past them without so much as a sidelong look.

He would make Washington pay for turning against him. It was not in his nature to forgive a slight, no matter how minor. He had been raised on the Bible and a leather strap, with an emphasis on the angry God of the Old Testament—the one who demanded eyes for eyes and ordered that all who bowed to the golden calf put to the sword. His country had made him a renegade—and, by damn, he was determined to be the biggest, nastiest thorn in its side. He would fight his country as relentlessly as he had fought *for* it—and with the same mercy he had shown the Injuns he had so diligently exterminated at Washington's command.

Drake paused for a moment to study the dead men lined up at the foot of the boardwalk. After three days they were beginning to stink and draw flies. He glanced up at the lowering sun and made his decision.

Come the dawn he would order his men to kill the women, then nail the doors to the church shut and torch it. Drake chuckled as he imagined the look on the president's face.

The woman wouldn't stop screaming. Even after Dawson climbed off her, she still kept shrieking. It was getting on Drake's nerves.

"Shut her up!" he barked. "I've listened to enough caterwauling tonight!"

"Yes, sir!" Barnes saluted. He drew his service revolver from his holster and stepped up to the poker table where the naked woman lay huddled, screaming into her hands.

The other members of Drake's Devils fell silent, their debauchery momentarily forgotten, upon hearing the revolver's report. The only other sound in the room was that of the player piano hammering away mindlessly at *My Darling Clementine*.

"What are you men looking at?" Barnes bellowed as everyone silently stared at the woman's body. "Ain't you never seen a bitch put out of her misery before?"

"You mean you put her out of *our* misery, Lieutenant!" Lewes laughed, toasting Barnes with an upraised bottle of rotgut.

"Ain't that right, boys?"

A ragged chorus of laughs rose from the men. The laughter of the women was noticeable for its absence. Then again, they hadn't done anything except scream, cry, groan, and beg for mercy for days on end. When the men weren't fucking them on top of the gaming tables, the captive women stayed huddled together like baby rabbits trying to keep warm. Whenever one of Drake's Devils felt the need, he would stagger up and simply drag one of them off to do whatever it was he wanted.

A few of their number were professional whores, but the rest were the mothers, daughters and sweethearts of the men lying dead in the street. The working girls tried as best they could to put themselves between the outlaws and the other women, but there were simply not enough of them to go around.

Drake watched the women weep and shiver in fear, scowling in disgust. As loathsome and primitive as they might be, he had more respect for squaws than he did white women. At least a proper squaw would kill herself before allowing herself to be raped.

As Drake's Devils once again resumed their monstrous revelry, another scream rang out. But this time it didn't come from inside the saloon or from a woman. Seconds later, Ferguson's body came flying through the batwing doors and landed on the sawdust-strewn floor.

Lewes stared at the halo of blood forming underneath his friend's head, his face drained of color. "Where's his ears?" he croaked, wiping his upper lip with the sleeve of his shirt.

Drake leapt from his chair and grabbed one of the women, a young girl who would have been pretty if not for the bruises on her face. The girl sobbed in fear and pain as he dragged her to the door of the saloon by her hair. Drake positioned himself in the threshold, using her as a shield, and pressed his pistol against her temple.

"I don't know who you are out there—!" he shouted at the darkness. "And I don't care!" He wrapped another length of the girl's locks around his fist, pressing her tear-stained cheek closer to the muzzle of his gun. "Pull another trick like that, and I'll have my men open fire on the whole lot! You hear me?"

There was a long silence, then a lone voice spoke from somewhere in the darkness: "I hear you, Drake."

He backed away from the open door and then roughly cast the sobbing girl aside. Whoever killed Ferguson must have taken out Powell as well, which meant that Drake no longer had the church. That left him with only the women in the saloon as bargaining chips.

"Captain—did you recognize the voice?" Barnes whispered.

Drake shook his head, preoccupied.

"Do you think it's the Army?"

Drake snorted and pointed at what remained of Ferguson. "Whoever did that ain't reg'lar Army. I'm bettin' on vigilantes."

"Vigilantes?" Barnes frowned. "How would they know to look for us here?"

Before Drake could answer, there came the sound of horse's hooves hammering against a boardwalk at full speed. Drake grabbed his gun and spun around in time to see the Devil himself come crashing through the front window of the saloon. Drake knew the man dressed in the black duster with the scarf thrown round his neck had to be the Devil because he had mismatched eyes—and the face of a dead man.

Satan rode a coal black horse with eyes that burned like coals snatched from the inferno's hottest forge. In his right hand, he held a pearl-handle revolver, in his left a shotgun, and between his teeth was clamped the reigns of his mount. The black horse landed on one of the flimsy gaming tables nearest the door, sending empty whiskey bottles and poker chips flying. The roughness of the landing, however, did nothing to shake the rider's aim. Within seconds Lewes, Childers and Dawson were dead, bullets lodged in their brains, hearts and lungs.

Realizing they were under attack, the remaining outlaws dove for cover and began immediately laying down fire. The women, forgotten in the confusion, ran for the backdoor of the saloon.

Lucifer glanced up at the wagon wheel that served as the barroom's chandelier. Ignoring the hot lead whistling past him like angry mosquitoes, he raised his gun and fired at the pulley mechanism. The chandelier crashed to the floor, killing the outlaw standing under it instantly. The six kerosene lamps affixed to the spokes shattered on impact, sending burning kerosene flying in all direction. Within moments, the saloon was on fire.

"You murderin' son of a bitch! I'll get you for what you done!" Detweiler screamed as he lunged from cover, burying the blade of his knife in the stranger's right leg. But to his amazement, the other man did not so much as flinch. The horse he was riding, however, closed its white, strong teeth firmly on Detweiler's throat, shaking him back and forth as a terrier would a rat.

Drake saw the Devil staring at him through the smoke and fire he'd brought with him from Hell. Drake was frozen, unable to look away from the pale specter as he made his slow, stately way toward him from across the burning barroom, the fire reflecting in his mismatched eyes.

Suddenly Barnes was there, shouting in Drake's ear, tugging on his arm. "Captain! We've got to get you away from here before the whole building comes down on our heads! Grunwald! Obermeyer! Help me get him out!"

Drake looked into his second-in-command's face, his piercing blue eyes clouded by confusion. "He's here to take me back."

"Take you back where—?" Barnes frowned in confusion. "To Washington?"

"No; to Hell," Drake replied.

Suddenly there was a loud groan and a burning timber came crashing down from the ceiling, blocking the Devil's path. Someone screamed, and Drake turned and saw the flames swallow Grunwald. Barnes grabbed Drake by the collar and dragged him through the shimmering curtain of fire toward the back door that the women had used to make their escape. A second later they were outside, coughing smoke out of their lungs and swatting at the burning cinders clinging to their clothes and hair.

Upon sucking in a lung-full of fresh air, Drake seemed restored to his usual vigor. "That son of a bitch double-crossed me!" he roared. "He sent one of his monsters after me!"

"Sir?" Barnes gasped, blinking in confusion. "I don't understand—"

"It is not your place to understand me, Barnes—only obey!" Drake shot back. "How many men are left?"

"Just Obermeyer and myself, sir."

"Then that will just have to do. We're saddling up and leaving right now."

"Where are we going, sir?"

"To settle the butcher's bill, Lieutenant."

It took Lynch a few hours to dig his way out from under the rubble of what had once been the saloon. When he saw the ceiling coming down, he dived under the bar, which saved him from getting his back broken or his skull smashed by falling rafters.

He looked down at his hands—the flesh covering them was reddened and blistered from the intense heat but otherwise whole. He touched his face, making sure that everything was still in its proper place. A large flap of skin hung from the side of his face like a piece of wet tissue paper, but outside of that he seemed to be intact.

As he stumbled out of the jumble of charred timber and burned bodies, he heard a shocked gasp. He looked up and saw a knot of townspeople standing on the nearby boardwalk, staring at him in horror. Lynch dusted the ash off his clothes as best he could, then smiled and tipped his hat.

"Don't mind me, folks," he said, smoke curling from his mouth as he spoke. "I'm just passing through."

Chapter Fourteen

AFTER LYNCH DUG HIMSELF free of the ruined saloon, he spent some time tracking down Alastor, who at least had enough horse sense not to stay inside a burning building. Once he had finished sewing the various bullet and knife wounds in his body shut and given himself an injection of the good doctor's marvelous elixir re-vitae, he was faced with the question of provisions for the journey ahead.

He waited until it was dark to sneak back into Newtonville and drag Powell's body from under the stairs of the church. When he first arrived, he'd been tempted to steal one of the corpses Drake had left lying in the street, but he was afraid of drawing the outlaws' attention to his presence before he was ready. Besides, they were already a little too ripe for his tastes.

Once he finished butchering Powell into easily carried choice cuts, he sat down for a much-needed meal. He figured Drake had a three-day start on him. But that didn't mean much to a man who didn't sleep and never got tired. Besides, it wasn't like the renegade was going out of his way to hide his tracks. Either Drake thought he was dead, or he didn't give a good goddamn that he was being followed.

At first Lynch wondered where Drake thought he was going. But as he followed his prey's trail across the plains, toward the towering peaks of the Grand Tetons, he realized that, for some reason, he was being lead back to the scene of his rebirth.

The cabin was in shambles when he arrived. The bookshelf had been knocked over, its cache of rare volumes and medical texts spilled across the floor like playing cards. The table was upended, its chairs reduced to kindling. The door that lead to Mirablis' secret cave stood wide open, sagging on broken hinges. Lynch hurried into the darkness on the other side of the threshold without hesitation. To his eyes, at least, the cave's shadows held no secrets, its darkness no mystery.

"*Doc! Where are you?*" he called out.

The only response to his call was his own voice echoing back to him. As he continued his search for the old man, he stumbled and nearly fell across a body sprawled on the cave floor. He recognized the dead man as Barnes, Drake's second-in-command.

He was the one who had knotted the rope that snapped Johnny Pearl's neck so neatly. He realized Barnes's face was staring up at him, even though the dead man was lying belly down.

Pompey lay a few feet away from the outlaw's body. The mute was riddled with bullets, but what finally snuffed out the second life of the doctor's faithful servant was the shot that parted his sinus cavity down the middle.

But if Pompey was dead . . . what had become of Mirablis?

Lynch got his answer when he reached the tank. The artificial womb's glass panels were smashed, and a huge puddle of elixir re-vitae was pooled underneath the structure. Mirablis's body lay face down in the greenish yellow fluid, blood seeping from a half-dozen bullet wounds.

Despite himself, Lynch cried out in alarm. He hurried forward and awkwardly knelt beside his creator. Lynch rolled Mirablis over, hoping against hope that he might still be alive, but his prayers were in vain. Though his wounds were still fresh, Mirablis' flesh had already taken on the chill of death.

Lynch sobbed as he cradled the dead scientist in his arms, rocking back and forth as the grief rose within him. As much as he had resented Mirablis' interference with his life—and afterlife—he had never wished the old man any harm. He clutched the body to his breast, mourning him as Johnny Pearl had never been allowed to mourn his own father, all those years ago.

"No—not like this—I didn't mean for it to be like *this*," he moaned. "I never meant for anyone but Drake and his men to die!"

There came the sound of a boot heel scraping against rock, and Lynch found himself staring at the muzzle of Drake's gun. Though he knew he was moments removed from his second and final death, all Lynch could think was how shabby the once-fearsome Captain looked.

The renegade officer still wore his cavalry uniform, but the company insignia and his officer's stripes were now missing from the shoulders and sleeves. His handsomely coifed red mane and beard was tangled and liberally shot with gray, the whiskers about his mouth permanently stained by tobacco juice and whiskey. His eyes still shone as brightly as the first time they met, but now they burned with madness.

"That's right. You were too late to save your master," Drake snarled, blood smeared across his lower lip and chin whiskers. "Still, the old bastard put up a hell of a fight—more than Barnes and Obermeyer were expecting, that's for sure. Or, rather, his pet monsters put up the fight." Drake waved a bloody hand in the direction of what was left of Obermeyer scattered about the cave floor.

"Where's Sasquatch?"

"You mean the Injun? When it realized the old man was dead, it hollered like a stuck hog and ran off into the cave. It's dead, too. Or will be soon. God knows I emptied enough lead into it."

"I don't understand—how did you know to come here?"

Drake laughed and spat a wad of bloody phlegm on the floor of the cave. "Don't play innocent! I know what that ungrateful sack of shit did! He didn't have no more use for me, once I was drummed out, so he sent you after me! Who was he to think he could treat me that way after all I'd done for him over the years?"

"What do you mean?"

"Who do you suppose it was who allowed that medicine wagon to travel unmolested by Injuns—or dissatisfied customers, for that matter!" Drake snorted. "Hell, I even provided him with bodies for those damn fool experiments of his!"

"Y-you mean you and Mirablis—you were working together?"

"Let's just say we had us a business arrangement. The old geezer paid me so he could get first crack at the spoils of war, as it were." Drake studied Lynch's face for a moment then gave a short laugh that sounded like a bark of pain. "You ain't shittin' me, are you? You really *didn't* know about me and th' old man. Huh! I guess Mirablis was right when he said this was all a big misunderstanding."

"Oh. There's no misunderstanding," Lynch said as he laid Mirablis body on the ground, his voice strangely calm. "I *am* gonna kill you, you murderin' Yankee bastard."

"You can try, you broke-neck freak," Drake snarled. "But better men than you have died tryin'."

Lynch smiled, his eyes glowing like stars in the gloom of the cavern as he got to his feet. "Be that as it may, Drake. But then again—I'm already dead."

The bullet struck Lynch's neck brace, knocking him onto his back. Drake moved forward and pointed the gun point-blank at the other man's head and repeatedly pulled the trigger, only to have the hammer click onto empty chambers.

"*Damn you!*" Drake screamed in rage, hurling the useless gun aside. He turned and fled as fast as he could, stumbling through the darkness toward the light that marked the open doorway leading to the cabin.

Lynch took his time getting to his feet. There was no point in hurrying after Drake. After all, where could his prey possibly go that he could not follow? Drake was a dead man and knew it. Lynch could afford to stalk him at his leisure—after all; he had all the time in the world.

Chapter Fifteen

DRAKE RAN THROUGH the cabin's single room, bursting through the door and into the open air. He was bruised and cut from slamming into rock formations in the dark, and he had a cracked rib from where the Injun freak had grabbed him, but he was alive—which was more than could be said for Barnes and Obermeyer. He had to get some space between him and that broke-necked son of a bitch. Once he had space, he could figure out a battle plan. But right now he had to grab his horse and ride.

Drake hurried toward the barn, only to come to a sudden halt upon seeing the doors standing wide open. The horses that he and the others had arrived on were lying on their sides. Standing in the middle of the fallen animals was a black horse, tearing at the flesh of the fallen animals as if it was grazing in a field of clover. The black beast raised its head and made an angry snorting noise as it pawed the ground, staring at him with glowing eyes.

The outlaw made a choking sound, then turned and fled on foot, following the narrow winding path that lead toward the top of the mountain. As he neared the first bend, he looked over his shoulder and saw the hanged man standing outside the cabin, watching him.

* * *

Lynch watched Drake run until he was out of sight, then fished out his pocket watch and Katie's braid. He sat down on a nearby rock and stroked his dead wife's hair, the time piece resting beside him with its case open. When five minutes had passed, Lynch snapped the case closed and returned the watch to his waistcoat pocket. He began walking in the direction his prey had gone.

Halfway up the mountain, Lynch noticed that the wind had grown considerably stronger. He paused to tilt his head back as best he could and stare up at the sky. There were clouds gathering overhead—growing larger and darker with every minute. He grunted to himself and returned Katie's braid to his breast pocket.

A few minutes later, the foot path disappeared, and Lynch found himself alternately hiking and scaling his way up the side of the mountain. Though there were plenty of natural handholds in the form of rocks and stunted shrubs, the rigid neck brace made it difficult for him to maintain his balance while climbing. He was within feet of the pinnacle when something wet and cold splashed against his cheek.

As he paused to wipe the raindrop from his face, a large rock struck him in the shoulder, sending him sliding ten feet down the side of the mountain. As Lynch struggled to regain his footing, a second, even bigger stone struck him squarely on the spine.

In the months since his resurrection, Lynch had forgotten what true pain actually felt like. He routinely suffered shootings, stabbings and being burned alive, much like anyone else would endure a scraped knee or bruised elbow. However, the pain exploding along his spine was so intense it was all he could do to keep from screaming until he burst a lung. As he lay there, groveling in agony, he could make out Drake's silhouette on the ledge above him. The outlaw looked like a wild-haired savage preparing to bash out the brains of his enemy.

"I'm gonna kill you, dead man!" Drake shouted as he lifted a small boulder over his head. "And this time you're gonna *stay* dead!"

As if to punctuate his statement, the storm clouds swallowed the sun. The winds howled like wolves scenting blood. Lynch stared up at his killer, awaiting the final blow that would return him to his wife.

Just then a crooked shadow rose up from behind Drake, and a

pair of mismatched arms encircled his barrel chest, lifting him off the ground as if he were a child. Startled, Drake dropped the boulder, which bounced harmlessly past Lynch, then sailed off the side of the mountain into the valley below.

"*Put me down!*" Drake screamed. "*Put me down, you red-skinned freak, or I'll yank your guts out your ass and feed them to you!*"

If Sasquatch heard Drake's threat, he showed no sign of it. The crazy-quilt Indian had his eyes shut and his head thrown back. Lynch could barely make out the sound of ritual chanting over the thunder. Suddenly Sasquatch's eyes flew open, and his gaze fell on Lynch's and held it. The giant smiled as best he could and mouthed the words "*Forgive me*" in English. Then there was flash of blue white light so intense that it transcended sight, followed by a noise so loud it sounded as if the mountain was cracking open.

When Lynch regained the ability to see and hear, the first thing he noticed was that his eyebrows were singed off. The second thing he noticed was that he was alone. He lurched to his feet, trying not to overbalance and slide even further down the side of the mountain.

He scoured the top of the mountain for signs of his friend, but all he found was a blasted patch of rock located roughly where Sasquatch had been standing. Lynch called his name over and over, but there was no answer except the distant rumble of the passing storm.

Epilogue

LYNCH KNEW HE SHOULD BE ANGRY about how he had been used and betrayed, first by Mirablis, who had been secretly in cahoots with his murderer, and then by Sasquatch, who had used him to lure Drake within convenient striking distance so he could avenge himself against the man who slaughtered his tribe. But try as he might, he could not bring himself to hate them. What was done was done. There was no way of changing the past, only learning from it.

He searched through the papers scattered about the floor of the cabin until he found Mirablis' private journals and the Frankenstein notebooks. The pages were yellowed and filled with cramped handwriting, most of it in a language he did not recognize, and included chemical and mathematical formulae. How was he supposed to decipher this in time to figure out how to make more elixir re-vitae before his supply ran out?

If the notebooks had proven somewhat disappointing, the steamer trunk at the foot of the old man's bed made up for it. Inside he discovered a variety of glass jars, in which various human body parts were suspended in elixir re-vitae. Lynch lost no time in tossing out the collection of hands, livers, hearts and genitalia, and then decanting the precious elixir into containers more suitable for transportation.

The last jar was also the largest—roughly the size of a three-gallon jug. As Lynch lifted it out of the trunk, he was surprised to find it contained an unborn child. A child with Katie's cheekbones and his chin. As he leaned forward, the child in the jar jerked, like a sleeper in a dream, and stuck his thumb in his mouth.

All it took was a small keg of black powder to seal off the entrance to Mirablis' underground laboratory and reduce the cabin to a pile of splinters. Once he was certain all traces of the scientist's existence had been obliterated, he hitched up Alastor to the old medicine show wagon. He climbed up onto the driver's box and released the brake. Without being told, the undead horse began to head toward the setting sun and a new beginning.

He had lived the life of the destroyer before and found it empty. Now he had a new mission in life—one that demanded far more of him than killing. It was up to him learn how to defeat the dark hunger that threatened to make him a monster, and find a way to decipher the old man's journals and help him change his nightmares back into dreams. As much as he missed his beloved Katie, and yearned to rejoin her, it was necessary to postpone their reunion. Somehow, he was certain she would understand.

After all, their son needed him.

Find out more about Nancy A. Collins at:
www.golgothamonline.com
truesonjablue.blogspot.com
hopedalepress.blogspot.com

Milton Keynes UK
Ingram Content Group UK Ltd.
UKHW040639131024
449481UK00001B/60